DON /GOJ

Return
or a
P

IST OF GOLD

TWIST OF GOLD
MICHAEL MORPURGO

CHILDREN'S LAUREATE

EGMONT

For Clare

First published in Great Britain in 1993
by Kaye and Ward Ltd
Reissued 2001 by Egmont Books Ltd
239 Kensington High Street, London W8 6SA

ISBN 0 7497 4687 4

10 9 8 7 6 5

A CIP catalogue record for this title is available from the British Library

Printed and bound in Great Britain by the CPI Group

FOREWORD

WHEN MY GRANDMOTHER GREW OLD AND could no longer play the fiddle because her fingers were so stiffened and gnarled, she used to tell us often of how the first O'Briens came to leave Ireland for California. Sitting in her rocking chair on the verandah of the old ranch house she had been born in and that she would allow no one to alter, she would tell us the story we all knew so well.

She would sit, her knees covered against the evening breeze in a scarlet cloak, a white moon-shawl over her shoulders; and around her neck she wore a wonderful golden torc that caught the red of the sun as it sank over the hills.

Although we knew the story almost word for word, we loved to hear it because she told it with such pride.

'My father was Sean O'Brien,' she would say. 'Your great grandfather he was and a finer man than he never lived; and he told me this story himself, so it's true – every word of it.' She would begin the same way each time she told the story, telling us of the Ireland of 1847 when the potato crop, the food of the people, failed yet again, stricken with a sudden blight that reduced the countryside to a pungent mass of black rot and left the people starving. In a small village in County Cork, Sean spent every waking hour in the desperate search for food to keep his mother, sister and himself alive.

CHAPTER 1

THE BOY AND THE DRAGOON SAT IN THE WARM drizzle on either side of the river. It was a close, still evening, and the flies were down. The boy knew he was there but ignored him as he had been instructed so often by his mother. He baited his hook yet again and cast it into the river. The Dragoon's horse stood with his legs in the cool of the water and drank tidily. The man sensed the boy's burning enmity; he had encountered it often enough before from the children of Ireland, but it hurt him none the less as it always did. He removed his heavy plumed helmet and placed it on the ground beside him balancing it against the bank. His scarlet cloak he threw aside on the ground behind him and then lay back on it, his head resting on his hands, looking over the top of his boots at the boy who sat rock-still on the bank opposite him. This way, he thought, he could pretend to be asleep and watch the boy at the same time.

The boy wore nothing but rags, like all the other children, and he went bare-foot. He was thin, but not yet as skeletal as some the Dragoon had seen. The signs of hunger were there already, the hollow cheeks, the stick-like legs and the dreadful white of the bones at the knees. It was the child's sunken eyes though that held the Dragoon's attention, fixed as they were in complete concentration at the point where his line lay in the water. His whole body was taut and waiting behind those eyes. It's as if his life depended on it, the Dragoon thought. And then, as he watched, the truth dawned on him in all its clarity. 'For Christ's sake, Will,' he said to himself, 'what are you saying? His life does depend on it. Look at him. You're looking at a dead child. In a couple of weeks, in a couple of months you'll be trotting along some dripping, leafy lane and you'll see a body lying muddy and still in a ditch. And it won't be just anybody's body, it'll be him.'

Impulse took him against his better judgement.

The Dragoon sat up suddenly, resting on his elbows, and called out. 'Son, hey son!' The boy looked up slowly, his face full of smouldering resentment. 'Son, I've some biscuits in my saddle bag. Would you like a biscuit, son? You'll not be catching any fish here, you know. I've been trying for weeks myself. The odd tiddly trout, that's all. Water's too low. You'll not catch anything, not in a month of Sundays. There's eels of course, but it's too light for eels and too early.' The boy glared at him as he spoke, his instinctive hatred mellowed already by the humanity in the man's voice. The Dragoon lowered his voice, deliberately trying to remove the threat from it. 'Look son. I won't hurt you. Honest I won't. I've a few biscuits in my saddle bag and I want you to have them – that's all. It won't cost you. It's a present. I've had my supper and you haven't had yours. You can talk to me, son. I don't bite you know. Look son, I'll tell you what. I'll throw you over three biscuits today – that's all I've got – and then I'll come back tomorrow with some more. How's that?' As he talked he stood up and moved over to his horse and unbuckled his saddle bag. He took out the three meal biscuits he had left and held them up in the air. 'Here you are, son. It's all I've got.'

The boy stood up slowly, his line still lying in the water, his eyes never leaving the Dragoon's hand. He spoke softly, but with not a trace of supplication. 'Don't throw them, mister,' he said. 'I'll come across.'

'Meet you half way, son,' said the Dragoon exhilarated that the child had spoken to him at last.

They met in mid-stream and the Dragoon looked down at the boy as he handed him the biscuits. 'Shall I come back tomorrow, son? Same time, same place? Will you be here, son?'

'Could be,' said the boy, holding the biscuits tight in his hands and smelling them as if to confirm their reality. 'Maybe I will,' he said.

'What are you called, son? What do they call you at home?'

'Sean,' said the boy, never for one moment taking his eyes from the biscuits. 'I'm called Sean O'Brien.'

CHAPTER 2

SEAN SUPPRESSED THE SURGE OF EXCITEMENT that bubbled within him as he approached the village. A fresh source of food was not something to be shared with anyone except with his mother and his sister, Annie. The village was silent, empty of people. Only the smoke from the chimneys betrayed any sign of life. But he knew they were all inside the cottages, those that had stayed, those that had survived. Every door was shut against the world. No dogs came out to bark at him, no children raced down the bracken track from the church, no pigs snuffled in the fuchsia-covered ditches. The dust bowls by the churchyard gate were still there – mud-puddles in winter – but in summer all the hens and cockerels in the village used to congregate here for their ablutions and talk noisily as they wriggled and squirmed in the dust. Sean could not remember now when it was he last heard the cry of a cockerel.

He turned away from the church before his eyes were drawn to the three red mounds in the farthest corner of the churchyard. He spoke to them as he began the long climb up the hill towards home. He spoke aloud because he knew that only they would be listening. 'Danny, Mary, little Joe,' he said. 'A few more of these biscuits and you'd not be lying out there in the ground. I tried, you know I did, don't you? I'll come over and see you later with Annie, like we always do.'

The cottage was like any other in the village, a low squat building of stone, but with the tallest chimney in Ireland standing proudly out from the thatched roof. The chimney was his father's particular pride and joy. Sean remembered well the building of the cottage all those years before. Every cousin and uncle from round about, every able-bodied neighbour was there that spring and within days there was a cottage where before there had been nothing. His father, still strong and splendid in the strength of his youth, had supervised noisily as he always did, but louder than ever for this was his house and it was expected. 'The higher a chimney is, son, the better it draws,' he insisted when they scoffed at his giant of a chimney. And when it was finished he sat upon it with a glass of poteen in his hand, the evening sun firing his ginger beard as he threw back his head and laughed with them for it was indeed a monster of a chimney. 'Truly a wonderful creation,' Sean repeated his father's words aloud, and the thought of him brought a smile to his eyes.

The latch on the door was stiff and heavy, so Sean stuffed the biscuits down his shirt-front to leave his hands free to open it. They lay together where he had left them that morning, but his little sister Annie had been as good as her word, and the fire was well built up and the house was warm. Annie sat up as he came in, but his mother could only turn her head slowly. 'Well, Sean dear?' she said. 'Is it a salmon that you're bringing us this time?' It was said with no bitterness and no blame, but in a voice drained of all hope.

'No salmon, Mother, but what would you say to a biscuit, Mother, a great thick oatmeal biscuit, and a present from the British army himself?' Annie threw her arms around his neck and hugged him as if she would never let go.

'Careful, Annie, you'll squash them. Not so bad for a brother am I?'

His mother struggled to raise herself up to her elbows. In the light from the open door Sean recognised the cold blue hand of starvation on his mother's face, the same pallor that had come over Danny, Mary and little Joe before they died. He had known it for some days now, so it came as no shock to him, but a terrible sadness welled up inside him at the sight of her.

'Are you speaking the truth to me, Sean?' she said, her words punctuated by a rasping cough that took hold of her and shook her. Sean held up the biscuits in triumph.

'There'll be one for each of us, Mother,' he said.

'Can I eat it all, Mother?' asked Annie, caressing the biscuit. 'Can I eat it all today?'

'Every bit, Annie dear. But eat slowly for 'tis manna from heaven. Thank the blessed Mary for it and make it last as long as you can. God bless us.'

'God bless us,' said Annie, crossing herself speedily. 'And can I not begin now?'

The three ate in silence and when the feast was over and every crumb recovered from the ground, they passed round the pitcher of water and spoke once more. 'Did you steal it then, Sean?' his mother said as she sank back exhausted. 'Did you steal it? Well, no matter if you did, 'twas well done. One biscuit for us is one less for them I suppose. And don't they owe us more biscuits than each of us could eat in a lifetime?' and she sat up again, suddenly frightened. 'They didn't see you, Sean? They didn't follow you home? Annie, go to the door. See if anyone's there.'

'Hush, Mother,' Sean said, and he put a hand on Annie's arm. 'Don't trouble yourself, Annie. There'll be no one there. I was given the biscuits, Mother, honest I was. A Sergeant of Dragoons he was and brought his horse to my river to drink. And I know well, Mother, what you said about not speaking to the soldiers, but he stayed by the river and would not leave; and I would not leave either. It was my river before he came and I would not move away for any Englishman. You wouldn't have me run away, would you, Mother? So I stayed and he stayed. But Annie, I wanted so much to catch a fish just to show him it was my river, that the fish know me better than they know him. And then for no good reason he offers me the biscuits and says I am to come back tomorrow for some more. I've never spoken to one of them before, Mother – but there was something about this one, he was different.'

'Don't you go near the place, Sean,' his mother said, heaving to get the words out before the cough came on her again. ''Tis a trap, sure enough. Don't go near the place. D'you hear me, Sean?'

'But Mother,' cried Annie, putting her arm around her mother to support her. ''Tis food, Mother. Sure there's nothing else left for us. We must eat anything we can live on. 'Tis only what you told us yourself, Mother. We must live, Mother. For Father's sake, we must live. Have you not told us often enough? If we do not eat there'll be none of us here when he comes back to fetch us. And he won't be long now, Mother, I know he won't be long. And we can live on Sean's biscuits, Mother.'

'Your father made you promise him something before he left. Do you not remember what it was, children? He said I was to be mother and father to all of you until he came back to fetch us. Do you not remember the day he came from Cork where he met the sea captain who told him of a paradise on earth where the sun shines through the winter and there's food enough for everyone and plenty? And do you not remember he said he would go there and find us some land to farm and then come back for us? And you remember he said that while he was gone you were to obey me in all things? And you promised him, did you not?' Sean and Annie said nothing. 'Three of my children, three of his children are dead now from the hunger. Will you tell me how I shall ever face him and tell him that? And am I to lose another, his eldest son, for the want of one biscuit? And have you not yet learnt never to trust a uniform? Do they not tumble the houses, and burn the villages and take what they want from where they want? And do you not remember your father's warning about them? Surely there must still be fish in the rivers and rabbits in the fields. They cannot have all gone. 'Tis a trap, Sean, 'tis a trap I tell you.' And she sank back to the ground and turned her head towards the wall. 'Sean my boy, you're a good boy. Your father will be proud of you. And when he comes home to fetch us I will tell him how you've kept us in food when there was no food – but I will not touch another of your English biscuits – I should die rather.'

'Don't say that, Mother,' Annie said, pulling the blanket up to her chin and kissing her softly on the cheek. 'Don't talk of it. Rest now.'

'We'll be walking down to the church, Mother,' said Sean. 'We've to say goodnight to Danny and Mary and little Joe. Will you be all right on your own for a while?' But his mother did not answer him.

Sean took Annie's hand in his as they walked down the path through the bracken, across the track and up to the church. They walked in silence for each knew what the other was thinking, and they would not voice the terrible fear they both had, for to do so would be to bring what they dreaded so much within the range of possibility.

'I'll find something else for her, Annie,' said Sean at last. 'You'll see – he will not have taken all the fish out of the river – I've heard them jumping further down. She'll be all right – you'll see.'

'I know she will,' Annie said. And then later, 'Sean, why does Father not come back to us? He said he'd be gone a year or so, and it's been near enough two years now. And he does not even write any more. Why doesn't he come for us, Sean?'

'They say 'tis a long way to America, Annie, and a

long way back. And it's a terrible big place when you get there. He'll be finding the farm for us and a place for us to live and that cannot be easy, can it now? 'Twould take time now, wouldn't it?'

'Sure it would,' said Annie. 'But I wish he'd come, Sean, and take us away from here before it's too late. There's the winter coming, and we've nothing put by to see it through.'

'He'll be back, he said he would, Annie. He'll come. And even if the winter does come, we'll manage well enough. Never fear, Annie, never fear. Now we've to pick enough fuchsia to cover the graves, so let's get to it.'

Every evening the two children wandered the hedgerows and the lanes and gathered all the fuchsia they could carry before making their way to the spot where their brothers and sister lay side by side in the graveyard. They were neither of them satisfied until each grave was a scarlet carpet of fresh fuchsia; it made the graves special and covered the shocking nakedness of the earth. They stayed in that place no longer than they had to, working almost feverishly in their anxiety to be gone.

'Will you go back to see your Dragoon?' Annie asked as they walked back home.

'I'll think on it, Annie,' he said.

'Can I come with you then?' she asked, taking his hand again.

'Sure you can, Annie, sure you can. But not a word to Mother now; we don't want to trouble her. We'll fetch in a few turfs for the fire, shall we now? There's plenty cut.'

CHAPTER 3

THE TWO CHILDREN APPROACHED THE RIVER with care the next evening. A fine misty drizzle fell and the grass was wet under their feet. They picked their way through a field of thistles and gorse and came to the spot where Sean had met his Sergeant of Dragoons the day before. They were early, deliberately so. Sean no more trusted the soldiers than his mother did. He had seen them too often putting people out of their houses, pulling down their roofs and driving them away when they tried to find shelter even in the ditches. He had seen them drunken, arrogant and abusive in town. He had no cause as yet to trust the Dragoon and he did not. They crouched behind a clump of thick gorse and waited.

The Dragoon came whistling on his horse down to the river, resplendent in his scarlet cloak and golden helmet and jingling as he came. He dismounted easily and patted his horse into the river to drink. 'I'm here, son,' he called out. 'I'm here and I'm alone and I've brought you some biscuits just as I promised.' He took off his helmet and scratched his tousled head, looking around him. 'Come on now, son. Why would I harm you? Here, look,' and he reached into his saddle bag and drew out a brown paper packet. 'I managed to find six of them, they're a bit old and a bit tough but better than nothing. Maybe you've someone at home who'd be in need of them. That's what I thought.' He stood at the edge of the river now, and suddenly laughed. 'Son, I was here before you were. I saw you come, and I don't trust you any more than you trust me. Why should I? And I'm beginning to feel a bit stupid talking to myself. I've got to be back in barracks within the hour. I know you're there, son, you and your little friend. So come out and show yourselves. I shan't harm you – that's a promise. Sean, there's not a breath of wind tonight and that's the second time I've seen that gorse bush tremble.'

Somewhat sheepishly Sean and Annie stood up and moved slowly out into the open. Sean had Annie by the hand, more he knew to reassure himself than anything else.

The Dragoon watched the two of them approach. The girl was a head smaller than the boy with long dark hair and strong high cheekbones. Less wasted than the boy, her face still had the look of a child about it. She too went in rags but wore a ribbon of green in her hair. 'Your little sister, is it?' asked the Dragoon.

'I'm not little,' said Annie. 'And our mother won't eat your English biscuits.' She was instantly on the offensive, as she always was when slighted. 'She said she'd rather die than eat your biscuits.'

'Hush, Annie,' said Sean.

'It's all right, son. I like a girl that speaks her mind.' The Dragoon waded out into the river. 'Perhaps if she won't eat my biscuits then she'll eat this,' he said, and he reached inside his tunic and drew out a small fish by its tail and held it up aloft. 'This,' he said, 'is no English biscuit. It's an Irish trout. Caught it myself less than an hour ago downstream. D'you suppose she'd eat an Irish trout? I mean, you don't have to tell her that I caught it, do you now?'

The two children stepped out into the river to meet the Dragoon. The stones were slippery under their feet and the current tugged at their legs. In days past, Annie would have skipped through the river with no difficulty, but there was little strength left in her emaciated legs and she needed Sean's hand to steady herself. 'Here are your biscuits, Sean O'Brien,' the Dragoon said. 'Don't drop them now, will you? And your mother's fish I'll give to the young lady here.'

'I'm not a young lady,' Annie said sharply, snatching the fish from him. 'I'm Annie O'Brien and my father says you've no business here, any of you. He says you're robbers and thieves, and Mother says so too. He's gone to 'Merica to find a place where we'll never be hungry again. 'Tis a valley where the sun always shines and there's no soldiers and no rents and he'll be coming for us any day now – he promised.'

'Did he now, and is your mother sick, Sean?' the Dragoon asked.

'Everyone's sick,' said Annie.

'She has the hunger,' said Sean quietly. 'But the fish will help,' he added, wanting to make amends for his sister's bluntness.

20

'Brother Danny's dead and sister Mary's dead,' said Annie. 'And little Joe died three weeks back.'

'I'm sorry for that,' said the Dragoon gently. 'Tell your mother from me that I'm sorry and that I shall do what I can for the three of you.'

'You'll be back tomorrow, then?' Sean asked.

'I'll try, Sean,' he said, crouching down and putting a hand on the boy's shoulder. 'I'll try to be here most days. But you won't tell anyone, will you, Sean O'Brien? Will you, Annie O'Brien? If you tell they'll lock me up and I'll never be able to come again. You promise, then?'

'We promise,' said Sean firmly. 'Don't we, Annie?'

'I will if he promises never to tumble our house and put us out,' Annie said. 'Father's money he sent us has run out and we've not paid the rent for a month or more, nor shall we be able to. Mother talks in her sleep about it, does she not, Sean?'

'I won't tumble your house, Annie, and I'll see to it no one else does, and that's my promise,' said the Dragoon, brushing the hair back from her eyes. 'Cook the fish slowly, my girl, won't you, else you'll burn away all the goodness.' He stood up to his full height again and straightened his helmet. 'Tomorrow, children,' he said. 'I'll be back tomorrow. Goodnight to you both.' And he turned and waded back across the river.

'Mister,' Annie called after him. 'Mister Soldier, is it not awful heavy having to wear such a hat as that?'

The Dragoon paused before he spoke. 'It's what's inside your head that weighs heavy, Annie O'Brien, not what you wear on it. Do you understand me?'

'No,' Annie said baldly.

'Why, Mister?' Sean asked, at last bringing himself to ask the question that had been troubling him since the day before. 'Why did you come? Why did you help us? No one else does.'

'Sean, I'm a soldier. I have been a soldier for over thirty years. I've fought the world over for my Queen and for my country – that's my trade and I do it well. But in this country I've seen and done things that turn my stomach with shame. Perhaps it's a way of saying sorry, do you understand, son?'

'I think so,' said Sean. 'I think I do.'

'Well, I don't understand what he's talking about,' Annie said, tugging at Sean's hand. 'We'd better be gone, Sean. Mother will be worrying, and it's getting awful dark.'

But they stood by the river until the glint of the

Dragoon's helmet disappeared into the trees, until they could no longer hear the jingle of the harness.

CHAPTER 4

FOR A TIME THAT AUTUMN, THE CHILDREN COULD almost believe that their tribulation was at an end. The Dragoon came back faithfully to the river as he had promised. He came not every evening; but more often than not, he would be there waiting for them on the river bank and whenever he came he never failed to bring them the biscuits. And each time he came he stayed that much longer to talk, until Sean and Annie began to look forward almost as much to being with him as to the food they knew he would bring. He would set Annie high on his horse, climb up behind her and splash through the shallows under the overhanging alders. Then he would ease the horse up over the bank and set off at a gallop through the bracken. 'Faster, faster,' she would shout, her fingers entwined in the horse's mane, her eyes crying in the wind. And they would thunder out over the field leaping every ditch and every gorse bush in their path. And on the way back, she would sing to him the songs she had learnt from her father and the Dragoon joined in where he could.

Sean would stay always by the river. The Dragoon had taught him the patient craft of eel fishing – the baiting of the hook (loach were best), the weighting of the line and the feel of an eel – and Sean would sit in the mist and gloom of the evening, his hand on the line waiting for the telltale tickle. And if the tickle turned to a bite he would strike fast, jerking the line viciously out of the water before the eel had time to wrap itself around the stones at the bottom of the river. 'One day,' said the Dragoon, 'I'll not be here to feed you and you must learn to live from the land. There's people dying in this country because they don't know where to look for their food. They've dug the potatoes for so long, they've forgotten. Eels are there in plenty if you can only catch them, and I shall teach you. A still, dark night with no moonshine, the feel of light drizzle on your neck and a black pool.

Then they'll come, you mark my words, Sean, they'll come.' And sure enough they did. They took an unconscionable time to die in the sack and skinning them was a slimy, nasty business; but most evenings Sean was able to bring back at least one eel for his mother.

They would eat their biscuits only in secret now and never again mentioned the Dragoon to their mother. She knew of course, but was too weak to protest. She caught their exchanged glances and sensed their conspiracy whenever she mentioned the Dragoon; but no one had come knocking on their door as she had feared and the crumbs she often saw on Annie's ragged skirt meant that her children were at least being kept alive.

As the weeks passed, she longed to meet this unlikely benefactor, not to thank him – she could never bring herself to that – but just to see what kind of Englishman it was who would feed her starving children.

The diet of eels, secret biscuits and blackberries kept the children alive and put strength in their withered limbs, but it was not enough to turn the tide for their mother who seemed to weaken day by day despite anything the children could do to restore her. Even when there was food enough, she would eat only a little of it and could not be persuaded to take more. She could feel the will to live being sapped from her and there seemed to be nothing she could do to stop her decline. Any lingering hope she still held that her husband might come for them in time was fast slipping away. The last letter had been over a year ago. She tried each night to keep clear and close the memory of the day he left them. 'I'll be back for you,' he had said as he kissed her hair. And then he was striding away down the track and out of sight, and the children watched in silence beside her. Only the dog cried, pawing at the door of the cottage until it opened and she bolted past the outstretched arms of the children who called out after her, 'Kate, Katey. Come back.' But she had gone after her master and never came back.

Death itself and the dying of it held no fear for her, for she knew with total certainty that she would be with the Blessed Mary and the Saints and that her dead children were indeed waiting for her on the other side. It was the parting from the living that troubled her. With the vast reserve of physical strength and determination that had mothered and fed five children at last exhausted, she had one duty alone in the days still left to her – to see that her children had at least a chance to escape. She would not allow herself to die until that was done. For the first time in years the common nightmare, the shadow of eviction, receded, to be replaced by a feverish resolution to see her children safe. She lay in the dark of the cottage and prayed for their survival.

It was cold that last evening as the two children sat on the bank with the Dragoon. Annie had been talking all evening because she could find no one to answer her. The Dragoon seemed to be distant from her and Sean was concentrating on catching the eels. The more silent they were, the more she talked and laughed. She could never bear silences between people. 'Keep your voice low, Annie,' the Dragoon whispered at last. 'And when you laugh, laugh softly, else those eels will laugh too as they shoot off down the river. An eel can hear as well as it can smell.' Annie was hurt, for never once before had the Dragoon reproached her for anything.

'Will?' Sean said suddenly. 'In your country, in England, do the people have enough food to eat?'

'The poor are always hungry, Sean,' said the Dragoon. 'Always have been, always will be – no matter where they are – but there are more poor living here and there is less food to go around.'

'Before the potatoes died,' said Sean, 'we had food enough, plenty of it. We went a bit short every year just before the new potatoes were lifted – summer time – but then there were always fish and the old hens and the berries to keep us going. Will we all die do you think, Will? Will everyone in Ireland die? When you go, Will, and the winter comes and there's nothing to eat, we'll all die, won't we?'

'I'm not going, Sean,' said the Dragoon. 'So stop that blathering. Keep your hand on that line and stop your nonsense.' Sean felt too that the Dragoon was preoccupied that evening, not unfriendly – he was never that – but he was solemn and serious and quite unlike himself. The children had become accustomed to his giant's belly-laugh, his long and jocular stories of far-off places, his expert juggling with the river stones and his handstands across the river. They had been able over the last weeks to set aside his uniform and all that that implied. Indeed, Sean had appropriated his sword, and Annie his helmet. Even now she sat beside him on the bank covered in his scarlet cloak with only her chin showing under his helmet.

''Tis awful smelly inside here, Will,' she said, taking it off. 'Shall I be washing it for you?' She wanted to be closer to him, to provoke him into chasing her down the beach as he had done so often before, a chase that always ended with her being first enveloped in his great arms and then tossed high into the air. But this evening the Sergeant of Dragoons sat silent and sombre beside them, and she felt suddenly a great need to comfort him. 'I'm cold,' she said, inveigling her way on to his lap and snuggling up against him. 'What's the matter, Will?' she said. 'Is something the matter with you?'

He was silent for a moment and seemed to be steeling himself. 'Sean, Annie,' he said. 'I have to see your mother. Will you take me to your house? I wouldn't ask to be invited, but it's important and I have to see her.'

'She won't speak to you, we told you,' said Annie. 'She hates the soldiers and every Englishman that ever lived, and she told us never to see you or speak with you again. She wouldn't let you in the house, Will.'

'She knows, Annie,' Sean said reprovingly. 'Can you not see that she knows? She says nothing to us because Will is keeping us alive and that's all she wants – but she knows. It's not Mother I worry about, 'tis the others in the village. There's some there that would kill a soldier on sight if they caught him alone. Soldiers never go into the village alone.'

'I know that, Sean,' said the Dragoon, and he put an arm around both of them, 'but it'll be dark soon enough and if it wasn't important I wouldn't ask you, would I?'

'What's happened, Will?' Sean asked. 'Are they coming to put us out of the cottage 'cos we haven't paid the rent? Mother always said they'd come one day. Is that what it is, Will?'

'Oh you wouldn't let them do it, would you, Will?' Annie cried, putting her arms around his neck. 'You'd never let them do that, would you? You promised.'

'Of course not, Annie, but it's not that – it's worse than that.'

'Then what is it, Will?' Sean said, looking anxiously up into his face. 'Nothing could be worse than that, could it? Could it?'

'I wanted to tell your mother first,' said the Dragoon. 'I didn't want to have to tell you, but I can see I must. You mustn't be frightened, promise me that. We send out patrols into the villages and towns round about, perhaps escorting grain to the towns or just to let people know we're here in case there's any trouble or looting. I've been out often enough myself on patrol, and what I saw only yesterday just five miles away confirms all the reports coming in from all over Ireland. There's a plague, a fever, call it what you will, sweeping this country, and it's coming closer all the time.'

CHAPTER 5

THE TWO CHILDREN LISTENED IN SILENCE. AFTER the hunger, after the deaths of their brothers and sister, nothing could shock them any more; but their time with the Dragoon had somehow taken them out of their misery and grief and given them hope once again. They understood only too well the implications of the fever – it had come often enough before and filled the graveyards. Annie cried quietly at the news, but Sean would not allow himself to weaken.

'What can we do, Will?' he asked. 'There must be something we can do.'

'I have to speak to your mother before I can tell

you that, Sean,' said the Dragoon. 'Will you take me now?'

They waited until it was nearly dark before setting off through the fields to the village, the two children perched high on the Dragoon's horse that snorted noisily as he climbed the hill past the church and turned up along the bracken path towards the cottage. Sean lifted the latch of the door and led the Dragoon in by the hand, whilst Annie ran over to waken her mother. 'We've brought someone in to see you, Mother,' she said. 'Don't be angry at us, Mother. Will is our friend. He's been kind to us and he's a good man.'

'He said he had to talk to you, Mother,' said Sean. 'So we brought him. He'll not harm us, Mother.'

The Dragoon had seen cottages like this before – the hard earth floor, the utter emptiness of the room, the neat stack of peat by the fire and a cross hanging over it, and not a chair or table, not a bed in sight. It was as he had supposed, no better, no worse. But here at least was a cottage where the spirit was not broken by the wretchedness of its inhabitants. The floor was swept smooth and clean and the fire well banked up. There was fresh bracken brought in for the bedding and the only smell was the welcome mustiness of the peat smoke. There was no squalor here, only abject poverty. 'Well, bring the man in,' came a voice from the blanket. 'What do you mean by letting him stand in the doorway, Sean? Bring him in by the fire – 'tis all I can offer you, sir,' she said, 'and that's little enough, to be sure, after all you've done for my children.' She fought to gain her breath and could not do so. She said no more, but stared intently at the tall figure that seemed to fill the small room as her husband had always done.

'Mother,' said Sean, bringing him in closer. 'Will has come to warn you, to warn us, that there's the fever in Ireland. It's close by and he's come to warn us.'

'There's always fever in Ireland,' she said quietly. 'There always has been. It follows the hunger, it always has done.'

'Ma'am,' said the Dragoon gently, 'this is a fever like no other. It wipes out whole villages. I've seen it, ma'am, with my own eyes. I've seen it and it's a terrible thing.'

'Sure 'tis a terrible thing, hunger is a terrible thing. Do they not know that, your English government? We ask for food, we beg for food and they send us work at ten pence a day, scarce enough to feed one child; and anyway there's no food to buy, so the people rise up and fight for it and they send soldiers to put them down. And still the landlord we never see wants his rent paid. Rent for what? And if you don't pay, the house comes tumbling down over your head and you're left to die in a ditch.'

'Mother,' said Annie. ''Tis none of it Will's fault. He's a good man, Mother, a kind man.'

'I know it, Annie dear,' said her mother. 'I never thought to see it, and I never thought to welcome an Englishman into my house, and you are most welcome sir, most welcome. But there's an anger and bitterness inside me and inside all of us that will hang over this land like a shadow for hundreds of years after we've all gone.'

'Ma'am,' said the Dragoon, walking over to where she lay and crouching down beside her, 'I can do nothing to put right all the great wrongs that have been done in this poor country. All I can do is to help you and your children. And there's only one thing to be done. You must leave, and leave now.'

'Leave and go where, sir?'

'To America, Ma'am. The children have been telling me all about their father, Ma'am. You could join him there. They're going from all over Ireland.'

''Tis a fine and wonderful notion, sir, but we haven't a penny to our name – not a penny. And don't be thinking that my husband left us destitute. He did not; he sends us all he can, but it's precious little and I've not heard from him for a long time now. We have no money, sir, no money for the passage and they'll not give you a ticket without it.'

'I have money enough, Ma'am, enough for the three of you. You can get a passage for as little as six pounds. A soldier's pay is poor enough, Ma'am, but it is regular and I always keep some by me. If I didn't spend it on this I'd spend it on the drink. It's not charity, Ma'am. Your children have become friends to me over these last weeks. They make me smile and laugh out loud and God knows I've done little enough of that since I've been over here. It's simple, Ma'am, they are my friends and I want to help them. You know and I know there's no hope here for any of you. If the hunger doesn't kill you then the plague will. I've seen it all over this country, Ma'am. Leave now and go to America – it's your only chance. There's a ship sailing from Cork on tomorrow morning's tide. If we leave now we shall be in time.'

'Annie,' said her mother. 'Sit me up against the wall so that I can see this man better.' But she was too weak for Annie to lift by herself and Sean put his arm under her shoulder to help. 'Sean,' she whispered in his ear. 'Can I trust him? Can I really trust him?'

'You can, Mother,' said Sean quietly. 'There's nothing to fear from Will – I know it, Mother.' And his mother kissed him gently on the cheek and stroked his hair. She put her head back against the wall and closed her eyes for several moments before she spoke.

'Leave us, children,' she said. 'Leave us alone. I'll be wanting a few words with your soldier friend here. The pitcher is almost empty, so run along the two of you and fill it for your old mother, will you now, and knock on the door before you come back in. And don't be listening outside. No questions, Annie, just do as I say.' And the children left, albeit reluctantly, closing the door behind them.

'Let's stay and listen, Sean,' said Annie once they were outside, taking his arm and pulling him back.

'We'll know soon enough what they're saying, Annie, and it wouldn't be right, would it? Would it now?'

'S'pose not, but I can't bear not being there.' And they walked on together in silence down towards the spring. 'Sean?' she said. 'If I ask you one question, will you promise on the Blessed Mary to answer me true, will you promise?'

'I know what you're going to ask, Annie,' said Sean, for she had asked it before and he had always managed to dissimulate and to console in his reply, but she had never asked him directly. Perhaps she had never dared until now.

'I'm old enough, I'm nearly eleven, and that's only three years younger than you,' she said. 'And she is my mother. I've a right to know.'

'She's dying, sister Annie,' Sean said softly. 'And that's the truth of it. You know it without me telling you. We saw it with the others, the way the colour goes and the way they don't seem to want food even if it's there. They were just the same and they died.'

'I knew it, Sean,' she said and she clung to him, crying quietly in her grief. 'So even if we go to 'Merica, she won't be coming with us, will she?'

'No, Annie, she's too weak to move. You saw her, she can hardly sit herself up.'

'And what will we do? Oh, Sean, what will we do? We can't leave her.'

'We'll see,' said Sean, struggling to keep himself from weeping with her. 'We'll see.'

And they spoke no more about it but dipped

the pitcher in the spring under the bracken and made their way back towards the cottage. Annie knocked quietly and they went in. The Dragoon sat on the floor looking into the fire and holding their mother's hand. There was the small tin box in her other hand, the one she kept on the mantleshelf over the fire.

'Come closer, children,' she said. 'Where I can see you.' Her voice was firmer now and her eyes steady as she looked up at them. 'What I have to tell you,' she said, 'you will do for my sake and for your father's sake. In this box you know I keep your father's letters to me. We've read the last one often enough together, haven't we now, children? Sure, we've all read it so often we know it word for word. 'Tis a fine letter, and do you remember he said he would soon be setting off from Boston to find us a home?'

' "I will be going as far West as the sun leads me",' said Sean reciting the words by heart. ' "I will be following the sun all the way to a place they call Grass Valley, California. 'Paradise on earth' that old sea captain from Cork called it and that will be where I shall go. And when I've found Grass Valley I shall build us a house with the tallest chimney in all

America, and then I'll be coming back for you and we'll all be together again. Be sure I shall come for you. Be sure of it and do not despair." '

'So that is where you must go, children, to Grass Valley, California,' she said. 'He wrote the letter from a great city called Boston – Hamilton Street, Boston; and that is where you must seek him first.' She closed her eyes and took a deep breath before she spoke again. 'I have told you, children, as your father has told you often enough, that a long, long time ago our family was a great family, rich in land, that we fought alongside the kings and everywhere we rode was our own. All that is left of our birthright now is the golden torc that belonged to the first of the O'Brien chieftains over a thousand years ago. So long as we keep it we will never forget who we are. And wherever the O'Briens go the golden torc must go with them – you know that well enough. You will wear it now, Annie, and carry it like a battle standard to America 'til you meet your father again.' And from underneath the letters in the tin box she took out a torc, a ribbon torc of thin beaten gold, and handed it to Sean. 'Put it round her neck, Sean. It will protect you both from the dangers you'll be facing.' She spoke fiercely now. 'I will not allow this family to be wiped off the face of the earth. I will not allow it, do you hear? Sure the torc is the very soul of the family. Without it we are nothing, d'you hear me now?'

'You can come with us, Mother,' Annie said. 'You could carry her, Will, couldn't you? We could make a stretcher. You must come, Mother, you must.'

'I shall be staying here for a while,' she said, 'with Danny and Mary and little Joe. Will says he'll look after me when he can, and Father Murphy is good to us all and will see to it that I'm taken care of. And when I'm better Annie, I shall follow you, and I shall find you, be sure of that.' Annie made to speak again but her mother would not allow it. 'You're always asking questions, Annie child. Will you never just listen? Will has promised me to see you on your way. He says he'll take you as far as Cork and put you on a ship for America. Saving your father, there never was a kinder man, I know that now. He was sent by the Blessed Mary herself, children. I prayed to her each night and she has answered my prayers. Never leave your God, children. Pray every night to the Blessed Virgin and trust her. Trust no one on this earth until you know them well. Be kind and be good as I've taught you to be and when you see your father tell him that I did all I could and that we shall be together again before long. Now you can kiss me once each before you leave.'

'But Mother,' said Sean. 'We cannot leave you here alone. We cannot.'

'Father Murphy will be here in the morning. 'Tis Sunday tomorrow and he'll come to say Mass with me early – he'll take care of me until Will gets back. Now get along with you. Will says you have to be in Cork by dawn if you're to be sailing on tomorrow morning's tide. You've not a minute to lose.'

Annie kissed her first and buried her face in her mother's shoulder. 'No tears, Annie, I will not have tears. You know how much I hate to see you cry. Now you look after your brother and make him wash – he never washes his neck. You'll be his mother now, for a while.' Sean knelt down beside his mother and kissed her gently on both cheeks. 'And Sean, my son, be sure you grow up fine like your father and be sure you find him. And remember the torc, children, lose that and the O'Briens are finished – it is our soul you carry with you. It is in your care now, the fortunes of the O'Briens are with you. Promise me you'll get it to your father.'

'We promise, Mother,' they said.

'Take them, Will, and be gone from here now. God bless you. Now go, please go.'

As the horse plodded slowly down the track and away from the village, Annie looked round for a last glimpse of the cottage, but it had already disappeared in the dark. She kept her eye on the white wisp of smoke that drifted up from the chimney until it too was swallowed by the night.

'Never look back, Annie,' the Dragoon said. 'Never look back.' The Dragoon walked alongside them for some while before he spoke again. 'D'you think there's room up there on that horse for me, you two? It's an awful long way to Cork and I'm a Dragoon, not a foot soldier. I'm not used to walking.' And he put his foot in the stirrup and swung up behind them, encircling them with his cloak and putting his arms around both of them to take the reins. 'We'll be all right, children,' he said. 'I'll look after your mother, and that's a promise. You're looking back again, Annie. You mustn't do it. Sean hasn't taken his eyes off the road ahead, and that's the way it has to be. Remember always that your father's out there in America and think what it'll be to see him again. Keep that in front of you and never look back.'

'Will,' said Sean, who trusted his voice now for the first time. 'Will, where is America?'

CHAPTER 6

THEY CAME INTO CORK JUST BEFORE DAWN WITH the town silent about them. The rhythmic rocking of the horse had long since lulled Annie to sleep, and even the echoing strike of the hooves on the road had not awoken her. It was only when the horse stumbled on the wet cobbles that she was dragged back into consciousness.

There was no sun that last dawn in Ireland, only the creeping grey across the sea; and with it the lights below them became the shapes of ships and clapping mastheads with the gulls screaming above them. The scurry of running feet on the quayside and the urgent blasphemy of men's voices were enough to tell the Dragoon that the ship was preparing to leave. He spurred his weary horse into a tired trot. 'She's making ready to sail,' he muttered to himself, 'but we'll make it, children, we'll make it.' And they felt his arm tighten around them as the horse lifted its head, pricked its ears and galvanised itself into a snorting, unwilling canter.

Captain Marcus Murray of the *Pelican* caught sight of the horse clattering down the quay towards them, the Dragoon's scarlet cloak flying out behind him. From the top of the gangplank he watched them dismount; an unlikely threesome, he thought. The Dragoon took off his cloak and wrapped it round the little girl, who seemed half asleep, and taking both children by the hand he walked up the gangplank towards the Captain.

'Captain,' said the Sergeant of Dragoons, straightening up so that he towered over him. 'I want the best quarters you have for my two young friends. I want two berths on the upper deck and I want these children looked after like royalty, like royalty, d'you hear? I could have bought tickets from the agents you send out into the villages, but they are a bunch of thieves and I'll not be dealing with such men.'

Captain Marcus Murray was always willing to sell any amount of passages on his ship, through agents or otherwise – it did not matter to him, provided he received the money. Twice already that year he had filled his 300-ton barque with wretched emigrants and made the lucrative crossing to Boston. Each time he had set off with twice the number the ship could carry, but he knew that 'natural wastage' would ensure that large numbers of them would never reach Boston. Dirty they may be, he thought looking down at his two new passengers, but not since the days of the slaving ships had there been a more profitable cargo than these emigrants; and what was more, there was also North American timber to bring back, so that his ship was never empty on the return journey.

'I have a full ship, Sergeant,' he declared, 'but if the price was right I could find room for these two. In my experience children eat the same as adults, and they take up as much room. I'll take them for £20 and not a penny less. Take it or leave it.'

'Captain,' said the Dragoon, stepping closer to him threateningly. 'I'll pay you your £20, but on the strict understanding that these children travel in comfort. I've heard often enough what your steerage passengers have to bear before they reach America. Under no circumstances will they travel steerage.' And he counted out the money and handed it over, but he did not release it into the Captain's hand just yet. 'Do I have your promise, Captain?'

'Sir, I am an officer and a gentleman,' said Captain Marcus Murray, smiling through his teeth, 'and a deal is a deal. I'll keep them under my personal supervision. You may be sure of it.'

'Very well, Captain,' said the Dragoon. 'I have to trust you, but my friends here will be writing to me from America, and they will no doubt inform me as to how you kept your promise.' And he crouched down and folded the two children close to him. 'Well, Sean and Annie, from now on you'll be on your own.' And he lowered his voice to a whisper. 'Keep the torc well hidden under your cloak, Annie, there are men who would die for that. Gold will turn a good man rotten, believe me, children. Keep your wits sharp, for it's all you have to get you to your father. And remember, never look back. And think of old Will sometimes, won't you? And write to me and tell me how you fare in California.'

'We won't forget you, Will, not ever,' said

Annie, clinging to his neck. 'And I'll wear your cloak for ever.'

'You'll grow into it one day, little Annie,' said Will, 'and until then it will help keep you warm.'

'Will you not come with us?' said Sean. 'Father would want to meet you, to thank you, I know he would.'

'One day perhaps I will come. Who knows?' the Dragoon said, straightening up. 'Now be gone with you both, and do up that cloak, Annie.'

'Will,' said Annie looking up at him. 'You won't let Mother die, will you?'

The Dragoon bent down and took her gently by the shoulders so that he could look into her eyes. 'Your mother's very sick, Annie, you know that. She's closer to death than she is to life, and she knows it. That's why she wanted you to leave without her. That is why she gave you the golden torc. She may die, Annie, and she'll go to heaven to be with your brothers and sister. That's all she wants now, now that she knows you're safely out of Ireland, away from the plague and the hunger and on your way to your father. I'll do everything I can to make her comfortable. She'll be warm and she'll be well fed; but I'm no healer, Annie, and I'll not give you any hope. You pray to your saints, Annie, and I'll pray to mine, that's all any of us can do, isn't it?'

'God bless, Will,' said Sean and he put his arm around Annie as Will walked down the gangplank and away from them.

As the ship stole out of Cork harbour through the glassy grey sea, Sean and Annie stood by the ship's rail and watched the Dragoon leading his horse slowly down the quayside.

'He's not waving to us,' said Annie. 'Why isn't he waving?'

'He said not to look back,' said Sean. 'Let's go to the front of the ship and see if we can see America.'

'Will we not see him again, Sean?'

'No, Annie, I don't suppose we will.'

'Nor Mother?'

'I don't suppose so, no.'

'Nor Ireland?'

'No,' said Sean. 'But we're going to America, Annie. We're going to find Father. Just think of what Father said in his letters, Annie. When he's saved up enough working on the railroad he's going to buy a farm of our very own in Grass Valley. Annie, 'tis hundreds of years since the O'Briens had land of their own.'

They made their way through the crowds of emigrants to the bow of the ship which was deserted. Everyone on the ship it seemed was on the land side leaning over the rails for the last glimpse of Ireland. The ship passed the bar of the harbour and sailed away from the sun and out into the choppy waters of the open sea. The wind sprang up quite suddenly and the sails clapped and cracked above them until the four-masted barque surged under them, ploughing into the waves and groaning with the effort of it. The spray stung their faces as they clung to the rail, wind-whipped, caught halfway between exhilaration and fear.

'I can't see it,' Annie shouted.

'What can't you see?'

' 'Merica,' she shouted. 'I can't see 'Merica.'

'Well, it's out there somewhere,' said Sean. 'Must be out there somewhere. We can't see it just yet.'

Blinded by the salt spray, Sean took Annie by the elbow and led her in amongst the crowds still gathered along the rail for that last glimpse of Ireland. The coast was still visible but with every minute that passed it merged more into the clouds on the horizon until at last no one could distinguish cloud-line from coast-line and coast-line from horizon, and everyone turned away in silence. Sean and Annie stood with them, suddenly aware of the step they had taken and how alone they were. They had left behind them all they had ever known and loved.

CHAPTER 7

THE PASSENGERS WITH THEM WERE A MOTLEY collection of humanity. There were babes in arms, entire families and aged couples. There were well-dressed folk in fine cloaks and hats, alongside paupers who stood shivering in little else but rags. But elegant or wretched, all suddenly seemed stunned to silence, for Ireland was gone and there was nothing ahead but uncertainty. Annie was tired and hungry and wanted only to find a place to lie down. She was just persuading Sean to look for the berths Will had spoken of when the ship's bell rang out and everyone was called to the main deck.

Captain Murray, with his crew beside him, looked

down at this new batch of emigrants below him and despised them. The sneer on his face was that of a cruel and greedy man and he made no attempt to disguise it. He was small in stature and thick-set in a blue long-tailed coat and a flat peaked cap. His eyes were hard and heavily overshadowed by thick, bushy eyebrows that joined above his nose. His great black side-whiskers crawled from his earlobes down to the corners of his mouth. He resembled more a gargoyle than a man. No one looking up at him at that moment could have felt anything but apprehension for there was nothing about his person that was either reassuring or warm. And when he spoke his words only served to confirm that impression.

'You'll know by now that my name is Captain Murray, late of Her Majesty's Royal Navy and Captain of this ship. Be sure you understand at the outset that I am the rule of law on board this vessel. I have the power of life and death over each one of you. Never allow yourselves to forget that. Until you leave this ship at Boston I am in effect your master, your lord and your king. I am judge and jury both. I brook no disobedience amongst my passengers and no insubordination. All food and water is strictly rationed, in case the voyage proves longer than expected. There will, however, be ample food and water, one meal a day at midday and this will be followed by an issue of water. Steerage passengers will not frequent the cabins nor the upper deck.' The murmur amongst the passengers was as much one of surprise as anything else, but for Captain Murray it smacked of revolt and warranted instant rebuke. He leant forward over the railings his eyes raking the passengers below him. 'Complaints on board this ship will be regarded as acts of mutiny. Step out of line and I'll have you in chains, on bread and water for a week. And my crew will tell you I don't threaten idly. This will be a disciplined ship, do I make myself clear?'

He was about to turn away when Annie spoke up. She had not really intended to. The words simply came out as they often did with her, and there was nothing she could do to stop them. 'Thoughtless' her mother had called her often enough; 'rash' was her father's word for the same thing; but either way Annie could not help herself. She spoke her mind as she had always done. 'Mister Captain,' she called out. 'Can you be telling me where we sleep, sir?'

There was a long, uncomfortable silence as the

Captain sought out the source of this impertinent interruption. Sean was exceptionally proud of his sister's courage – he always had been; but he was concerned now by the attention she had drawn to herself.

'You'll be the little tinker the Sergeant of Dragoons brought on board,' said the Captain, nodding slowly. 'You'll accompany my First Officer, Mr Blundell here, to my quarters and I shall see what can be done.' Sean sensed the implied threat in his last words.

Mr Blundell was a broad block of a man whose tightly curling hair was greying at the temples. Sean noted he had sad, serious eyes that belied his rough exterior. They followed him through the dispersing passengers and down the companionway to the Captain's cabin. Sean and Annie were too busy looking about them to worry about the impending interview. Sean decided that ships were built more for children than for grown men as all the ceilings were so low. Mr Blundell had to bend double as he stepped into the Captain's cabin and ushered them in. The Captain sat behind a long wooden desk with brass handles that was covered in charts. He was studying them as they came in and did not look up.

'Vagabonds and tinkers,' he said gruffly, almost as if he was speaking to himself. 'Vagabonds and tinkers do not sleep in my cabins, no matter how much your Sergeant paid me.' And he looked up at them suddenly, walked around the desk and inspected the children minutely, looking them up and down and shaking his head in disgust. As Annie turned her head to look up at him the cloak around her neck became unfastened, revealing the gold torc. She fastened it quickly, but not quickly enough. The Captain's eyes narrowed suddenly as he caught sight of it. He reached out to touch it, but Annie, already burning with resentment, drew back and struck out at his hand, her sharp bony knuckles catching him across the wrist.

'A wild little tinker that needs taming,' said the Captain, rubbing his wrist. 'Less than an hour on board and you've already been thieving. We've had your kind before and we know how to treat you. Ireland's full of thieving little tinkers. Either you stole it on board or you filched it on shore before you came on board. Either way the punishment is the same. And don't attempt to deceive me. Your feigned air of puzzlement does you credit, but I have never yet known an Irishman who has not the morals of a rat.

Tinkers, the lot of you. You'll take off the necklet and place it on my desk. Do it or I shall be forced to ask Mr Blundell to remove it.'

'Necklet?' Annie said.

'Necklet, necklace, call it what you will, but take it off this instant.'

'Sir,' said Sean, trying to control the rage in his voice. 'Sir, the torc is ours. It has always been ours. It belongs to our family. 'Tis the most precious thing we have, the only thing we have, and we did not steal it, sir.'

'You people. You have such minds, such imaginings,' said the Captain darkly. 'You are the bottom of the pile, the sweepings of the world, and yet you seem to believe that everyone else around you is a fool. I am no fool, tinker boy. You came on board my ship barefoot, dressed in nothing but rags – one good cloak between the two of you – and you claim that the gold necklet she's wearing is your own. Does it sound credible, even to you?'

'He will not have it,' said Annie, backing away from the desk. 'He will not, he will not.'

'I could always throw your brother in irons, tinker girl,' said the Captain darkly. 'Is that what you want? For that is what I shall do, be assured of it.

A week in irons on bread and water, and another week after that if you like. Oh I know little girls, even Irish girls, do not steal, not generally. It was your brother that stole it, wasn't it?'

'No, no,' cried Annie. 'It's not true, it's not true.'

'If you were to give me the necklet,' the Captain went on, wheedling now rather than bullying, 'I shall see to it that your brother is not thrown in irons. He'll be punished of course. Thieves and vagabonds must be punished, but I'll not throw him in irons. Well, what do you say?'

'Best do like the Captain says,' urged Mr Blundell from behind them, in a manner that was at once both firm yet reassuring.

The two children looked at each other, both recognising the futility in further resistance. 'Do I have to?' Annie asked, and Sean nodded. Annie unclasped the torc carefully and laid it on the table in front of the Captain. 'It belongs to us,' she said, her eyes full of tears that she would not allow to flow. 'It will always belong to us. And Father says anyone who steals it will be cursed to the day they die.'

The Captain and Mr Blundell gazed down at the golden torc that lay on the unrolled charts, both strangely reluctant to touch it. 'A little witch, she is,' laughed the Captain. 'I'm not one who believes in curses, tinker girl. Your brother will pay for his thieving through labour, hard labour. You will be employed for the duration of the voyage as ship's boy under Mr Blundell's personal supervision. One transgression, tinker, and you'll be in irons 'til we reach Boston, and at this time of year with the autumn gales, that could be a long, long time. Now get them out of here, Mr Blundell. Take them to steerage where they belong.'

Annie's pent-up fury was quite evident to Sean in her tight lips and tear-filled eyes, so he hurried her quickly out of the cabin in case her self-control failed her and landed them in even more trouble. She said nothing until they were once more out on deck.

Mr Blundell led them across the deck, talking as he went. 'Take my advice, little children,' he said, striding ahead of them. 'You keep out of the Captain's eye-reach, both of you. He's a monster when he's roused, take my word for it. It's this ship, it's this damned ship and this rotten trade. He's a man with a twisted soul. Keep out of his eye-reach I tell you.' And he pointed the way down the companionway towards the lower deck. 'You'll find steerage down there,' he said. 'All the berths are taken by now, but you'll find a space on the floor somewhere. Take my advice, children, and spend as little time down here as possible. You'll see why. And you, boy, you present yourself to the ship's galley at dawn tomorrow morning, first light.' And he left them.

CHAPTER 8

''TIS ALL MY FAULT, SEAN,' ANNIE SAID WHEN HE had gone. 'I can't for the life of me stop my mouth speaking when I have something to say. And look what's happened now. The torc is gone, and how are we ever to get it back from that man?'

''Tis not the end of it, Annie,' Sean said. 'If I'm to be ship's boy I'll be working often enough close to the Captain I shouldn't wonder, and I can keep an eye out for it, find out where he keeps it. Never you fear, Annie. We'll have it back before long. We've had it for over a thousand years, and I'll not be the O'Brien that loses it.' But although his words were full of determination and confidence, quite enough to convince Annie, he himself was less sure he could fulfil his prophecy. He knew it would be neither easy to steal it back nor to hide it after he had done so.

They made their way down the companionway to the steerage deck that was from end to end a long, long dormitory. It was a scene of abject misery with the emigrants huddled together in groups, some whispering furtively and others whimpering as the roll of the ship turned their stomachs. Many of the children were already stretched out on the few double berths – crude constructions of wood, each with a thin mattress on a slatted base. The only natural light came down the companionway from the daylight above, so that the remoter recesses were only dimly lit with swinging, guttering lamps that cast more shadows than light. A baby cried relentlessly up against her mother, who rocked her too urgently to send the child to sleep. And as she cried others cried too, setting up a plaintive, pitiful wailing that reflected the misery every one of them felt as they looked around at the dungeon that was to be their home.

Sean picked his way carefully through their fellow emigrants followed closely by Annie. A few attempted to acknowledge them cheerfully, but most ignored them, so wrapped were they in their own wretchedness. One child they passed, curled up on one of the berths with two other small children, moaned continuously. ''Tis the malady of the sea,' Sean heard someone whisper. 'It will pass.'

Then like a shaft of radiant light in the gloom came the gentle tones of a fiddle, slow at first and tentative: but as the people hushed about them Sean and Annie picked out the unmistakable rhythm of a jig, and suddenly the feet began to tap everywhere and the hands to clap and the pit of misery was miraculously transformed. Smile met smile and despair seemed to evaporate. One old lady was on her feet in a trice, her heavy skirts lifted above her ankles, her feet flicking out over the boards, toes pointed prettily in the proper manner. The children on the berths sat up and forgot their heaving stomachs and even the babies stopped their crying, soothed and comforted by the warmth of the music. Still no one could see the fiddler himself, who must have been hidden beyond the arc of the furthest lamp, but that seemed not to matter for when he had finished playing they clapped and cheered him until he appeared shyly from the shadows and took his bow quickly before retiring once more. From just this glimpse the children could see he was a tall, gangling youth in whose hands the fiddle looked like a toy. He held up his fiddle to acknowledge the applause as if the fiddle deserved it more than he.

He was putting his fiddle away in its case when Sean and Annie came upon him in the darkest corner of the steerage deck. There was beside him an area of floor just about wide enough for the two of them to lie down.

'I'm as thin as a rake,' he said. 'Plenty of room here if you'd care to join me, and I'm thinking there's nowhere else for you to go, is there now? I know well enough for I have been up and down a few times and there's not enough room to swing a mouse, let alone a cat. You can't see a lot at first, but your eyes soon become attuned, do they not? And since we'll no doubt be sleeping much of the time, it won't matter a lot, will it now? And it's snug enough in the corner here – no one to pass by us and disturb us. And I've enough room to play my fiddle and that's all that matters. My name is Liam Donnelly – I'm from County Sligo bound for Boston like yourselves. "Fiddler Donnelly" they call me 'cos there's not a lot I'm good at except playing my fiddle, but I'm mighty good at that, best in all Sligo, though I say it myself.

I'm a modest sort of fellow, as you can tell. And who might you be?'

'I'm Annie O'Brien, and he's my brother, Sean; and I'm hungry,' Annie said sitting herself down beside him.

'She's always hungry,' said Sean apologetically. 'I'm never hungry 'til she speaks of it, but then I'm always hungry 'cos she never stops speaking of it.'

'Well, we'll not be having a feast tonight by the look of it,' said the Fiddler. 'I've known more hospitable men in my time than our ship's Captain, have you not? I don't like the look of him at all, not at all. But I've half a loaf of bread with me – 'tis all I have, that and my fiddle. My fiddle you cannot eat, Annie O'Brien, but you're welcome to share my bread. We'd best be quiet about it though, for there's some hungry mouths around here and I've not enough for the feeding of the five thousand.' He spoke as he played, in soft tones and in a manner that seemed to calm those around him. There was a smile in his voice.

The bread was hard and stale, but that was better because each mouthful could be worked on and savoured for longer. At last, when they had finished picking the last of the crumbs from their clothes, the

Fiddler spoke once more. 'Now if I'm not mistaken, and I'm not often mistaken, you'll be the two children the Captain sent for, is that right?'

Annie was about to launch into the entire story about how they had lost their precious torc, but Sean interrupted her before she could begin. No matter how likeable the Fiddler seemed, he saw no reason to trust a man on such a short acquaintance. 'He needed a ship's boy,' he said, 'that's all it was. I've to be up at first light and report to Mr Blundell. He's the First Officer and not a bad sort at all, by the look of him.'

'Is that what it was?' said the Fiddler, and he said no more about it. 'Can you by any chance play the fiddle, Sean O'Brien?'

'A little,' said Sean. 'Father taught me a little, but I can barely make a tune out of it.'

'Then you shall learn, Sean O'Brien, for I shall teach you,' declared Fiddler Donnelly. 'When I reach Boston that's how I shall be making my living. I shall teach the fiddle to every American that wants to learn it. I know every Irish tune that was ever written or played or thought of. It would be a privilege and a pleasure, Sean O'Brien, for me to teach you. It would assist my prospects greatly if I could be practising my teaching on you during the voyage. I would not force it on you, Sean, but I think perhaps you would like it. We have a long and tedious voyage ahead of us and I would teach you all the songs and dances, every Irish tune I know so that your soul would sing with them for the rest of your life. After a bit, you know, you don't even need a fiddle, you know them so well you can play them in your mind over and over. Sure 'tis almost as good that way and not half so much trouble.'

'And what about me, Mister Fiddler?' Annie asked petulantly. 'Can I not learn too? I'm not that much younger than he is.'

'Certainly, Annie O'Brien,' said the Fiddler, 'but we've only the one fiddle between the two of us. So instead I shall teach you to dance. A girl like you was born to dance, Annie. You shall dance and Sean shall play. How's that?'

'Perfect,' cried Annie, and she clapped her hands in delight. 'When we see Father again I shall be able to dance for him and Sean to play. He'll love that, and Mother would be proud of us, would she not, Sean?'

'She would, Annie, she would,' said Sean.

'That's settled then,' said the Fiddler. 'You shall be Fiddler Donnelly's first pupils.'

'Are you on your own, Mister Fiddler?' Annie asked suddenly.

'Not any more,' said the Fiddler, smiling down at her. 'Not any more.'

CHAPTER 9

FOR THREE WEEKS OR MORE OUT OF CORK, FAIR winds and fine weather smiled on the *Pelican*. She made good headway in seas gentle enough not to alarm the emigrants, almost none of whom had ever set foot on a boat before. The early seasickness seemed to finish as they found their sealegs. The warm days enabled the steerage passengers to leave the crowded squalor of the lower deck and to explore the length and breadth of the barque.

To begin with the food was adequate. The one meal for those with no money – and that was most of them – was a poor affair of salt meat, rice and oatmeal biscuits, but it was adequate; but there was much bad feeling in the ship that those with money could pay for as many meals as they wished. The expectations of the steerage passengers were not high. Many had long since forgotten the taste of good food, so leathery meat and stale biscuits caused only muted complaint; but the shortage of water was already proving uncomfortable. The daily water ration was ladled out into their cans from the barrels on deck, but only the cabin passengers and those at the front of the queue could be sure of their supply for the day. The sailors who supervised the issue of water and food were often as abusive and violent with the poorer passengers as they were ingratiating to the cabin passengers.

However, Sean's punishment proved to be a blessing in disguise. Certainly, Mr Blundell worked him hard. He fetched and carried from the hold to the galley, scrubbed every inch of the decks, served the Captain his meals in his cabin, scoured and scraped in the galley until his arms ached with the work of it. But his time in the galley and in the hold was not wasted. He came to know where every scrap of food was stored. In time he came and went as he pleased for he was trusted totally by the crew and eventually by Mr Blundell himself. They, of course, had three good meals a day, as did the Captain himself, so that Sean felt not a shred of guilt if some small proportion of their food disappeared from time to time into his pocket. 'Our little extras,' Fiddler Donnelly called them, and even Annie understood the importance of absolute secrecy. Were Sean to be caught pilfering, they knew the punishment would indeed be terrible. So a conspiracy of silence bound the three firmly together and kept them somewhat apart from the other passengers.

Mr Blundell proved to be a fair man, protecting both the crew and passengers from the excesses of his Captain, so far as this was possible. Without him there would have been many occasions where smouldering mutiny might have turned to flame. Many a time he was able to come between the passengers and the Captain when they were threatened with dire punishments for daring to complain.

To begin with, Sean made no mention of the torc or its whereabouts, but when after a week or two he ventured to ask about it, Mr Blundell said it was not the time to trouble the Captain with such matters, but he would see what he could do. Sean had been able to search every corner of the Captain's cabin in the course of his duties, but without success. There was a great leather chest in the corner of the cabin that was always kept locked fast, and after many days' fruitless searching everywhere else, Sean decided the torc must indeed be hidden in this trunk. He did find a key once in the Captain's coat pocket, but it did not fit the lock. He continued to search the cabin whenever the chance arose, even when he knew there was little point in doing so.

It was out of desperation that he decided at last to tell Fiddler Donnelly one evening about the torc. After all, he thought, they had known him for more than three weeks now and he had proved himself a good friend to them both. Annie could already dance as if she had been doing it all her life, and every minute he was free from his duties as ship's boy Sean had spent in fiddle practice with him. Annie had already told him about their mother and Danny and Mary and little Joe and all about Will. Why not trust him with this last secret?

They were sitting cross-legged in their dark corner when Sean at last spoke up. When he had finished the story, Fiddler said nothing for a moment, then, 'You must get it back, Sean,' he said deliberately. ''Tis too precious a thing for you to lose, and that to a rogue like Captain Marcus Murray.'

'But how?' Annie asked. 'He's looked everywhere for the key, have you not, Sean?'

'There's more than one way to open a lock,' said Fiddler. 'You cannot go in there and knock the Captain over the head and pinch his key, can you now? And even if you did so and managed to find the torc, they would be bound to seek you out and take it from you again. So 'tis best to leave it where it is for the moment, is it not? I mean, it can't walk away, can it now? You have to be a good ship's boy, Sean. The harder you work the more they will trust you and the more careless they will become. You must become one of them, so that they think of you like a piece of furniture. You've done well enough already, Sean, but take great care. Do nothing to arouse suspicion. Never hurry – that's the secret. Before he died my father was, amongst other things, a poacher – 'twas the only way to bring us enough to live on – and that's what he told me. Never hurry. We have maybe a month to unlock that chest, and a month is a long time.'

The next day came the first of the great Atlantic storms that took the barque and hurled it from one great wave to the next. She rolled like a barrel in the churning seas, the cruel wind whistling through the rigging and teasing at the sails. The Captain, much given to strutting his decks like a peacock in the fine weather, was conspicuous by his absence now and kept to his cabin. It was Mr Blundell who held the crew to their tasks, sending men time and again up aloft into the rigging to gather in damaged sails. Sean spent little time in the galley now, but manned the pumps for hour after hour in the pitch dark of the hold, knee-deep in water, in a desperate attempt to keep down the level of water. For three terrible days that first storm lasted and Fiddler played until his fingers curled with the cold. But it was enough to lighten the darkness of the nightmare the emigrants were living through. Annie blew on his hands to warm them whenever he paused, for nothing but his playing could stop the children from their screaming.

Try as they could to pump out the hold, the water rose inexorably, spoiling the last of the fresh food taken on in Cork. Worse still, half a dozen water barrels broke loose and crashed against the timbers before they could be lashed back. By the time the storm left them, over half the food and water remaining was lost.

'You see, boy,' said Mr Blundell to Sean as they

pumped out together after it was all over. 'Look around you. The hull leaks like a sieve. Another storm like that and we'll none of us see Boston alive. And she's no better up top. The rigging's rotten right through. I told the Captain two years ago it all needs replacing, but he won't do it. He'll not spend a penny of his ill-gotten gains. We've food for two hundred passengers and there's three hundred or more on board. I'm sick to the stomach when I think of it. Between you and me, my boy, this is a rotten hulk of a ship that plies a rotten trade. This is my last time. I'm signing off at Boston. I'll not have any more of it. But I fear there's worse to come yet, boy, worse to come. You mark my words.' And he said no more.

For a while there were no more storms, but the one great storm was enough to finish the weakest of the passengers, an old lady from Donegal going out to join her son in Boston. Deprivation before the voyage, incessant cold and damp on the ship and lack of good food were to be the death of her. She contracted dysentery and was buried at sea. Sean and Annie stood with Fiddler on the deck and watched her thrown overboard sewn up in a cloth that was weighted with a stone. And she was just the first. As the weeks passed and the food and water dwindled, dysentery set in and spread like wildfire through the steerage passengers, taking with it the weak, the very young and the very old. The stench below decks was nauseating by now despite desperate efforts by many of the emigrants to keep it clean. Now all those that were strong enough would rather pass the day out in the cold of the open deck than remain below in a place so rife with infection.

Sean's secret supply of purloined food kept his sister and Fiddler just fit enough to survive those terrible days. Hunger, of course, was not new to any of them, but with each day that passed, the food became more contaminated and uneatable. Through it all, Fiddler kept playing and not a day went by without a fiddle lesson for Sean, no matter how tired he claimed to be, or a dancing lesson for Annie, who was never too tired it seemed. Her insatiable prattle and irrepressible effervescence were the main source of inspiration for the young fiddler who was often tempted to lie down and curl up in his misery. She was the oil to his lamp, although she never knew it.

CHAPTER 10

CAPTAIN MARCUS MURRAY WAS AS GOOD AS HIS word. In the midst of this wretchedness, he enforced his regime ruthlessly. A farmer with a family of six protested one morning that if they did not receive more food none of his children would survive the journey – one had already died. The Captain had him clapped in irons and put on bread and water for a week for his temerity, and there were no more complaints after that. The people did not lack courage, but they lacked the physical will to resist. Hunger and thirst were fast sapping their strength. As the man was chained up in the hold, Sean noted a look of utter disgust on Mr Blundell's face. His jaw muscles were clenched in fury and the look he gave the Captain after it was all over left no doubt in Sean's mind any more that Mr Blundell was at heart a good and kind man, and a potential ally.

Sean had not forgotten the golden torc, but with disease and fever spreading through the ship and the certainty that food would be more and more scarce as they neared America, survival had become the first priority. In the end it was Mr Blundell who first mentioned the torc. Sean was alone in the galley scouring the pots when Mr Blundell came in. For some moments he said nothing, but made as if he was inspecting the cleanliness of the pots and pans. And when he did speak at last it was a prepared speech and delivered as such. 'Sean, my boy, I've something on my mind that I want to tell you. I've known you a month or more and know you to be a good lad. You've worked hard, taken your punishment without a grumble – not easy since the punishment was unjust in the first place.' Sean looked up at him, but Mr Blundell looked away quickly. 'I know you're not a thief, my boy, known it from the beginning. I know that the necklet rightly belongs to you and your sister, and I shall endeavour to put it right, my boy, be sure of that.'

And he went out before Sean could say anything in reply.

Some days later, as the ship moved slowly through a still sea, Sean was once again set to scrubbing the decks – it had been the first opportunity for some time to do so and they were slippery and filthy. He was humming 'The Wild Irishman', one of the jigs Fiddler Donnelly had taught him, when he found himself grabbed roughly by both shoulders and dragged along the deck and down the companionway to the Captain's cabin.

'God damn your soul,' the Captain shouted, his face red with fury. 'I'll rope's-end you, I swear I will. Once a thief, always a thief.' Sean looked about him and saw the leather chest with its lock snapped off, the lid raised up. He caught Mr Blundell's eye and sensed at that moment that he had a part to play. 'I swear, if you don't tell me where you've hidden it, I'll rope's-end you till you drop.'

'Hidden what, Captain?' Sean asked. 'I don't know what you mean.'

'Captain Murray, Sir,' Mr Blundell said, stepping forward. 'To flog the rogue would set the other passengers in revolt. But as ship's boy we could send him aloft into the crow's nest – it would be seen as part of his duties. It would be mighty unpleasant up there and I fancy 'twould change his mind somewhat.'

'Very well, Mr Blundell,' said the Captain, after a moment of hesitation. 'You'll see that he stays in the crow's nest and remains there until I call him down. A few hours up there in this cold might loosen his tongue. See to it, Mr Blundell.'

Once out on deck Mr Blundell took him by the scruff of his neck and led him towards the rigging. But the manner in which he spoke belied the roughness of the hand on his collar and confirmed that Sean's instinct was justified. 'I thought he would sentence you to chains and bread and water, but you'll be all right, I'll see to it. It's the only good rigging on the ship, my boy, you'll be safe enough if you take care. As you climb, don't look down whatever you do. And see that you always have a good grip with both your hands before you move your legs.'

'The torc?' said Sean softly. 'You have it, then?'

'It's safe, boy. Don't worry about it. I'm a man of my word if nothing else. The Captain will relent as soon as his wounded pride is healed, and I shall heal it fast. Flattery does wonders for Captain Marcus

Murray. You'll be up there for a day or so – that's all; and if I've done my calculations right we shall see the coast of America before that. Take this, quickly,' and Sean felt a small flask being pressed into his pocket. 'It'll help to keep the cold out, my boy. Go easy on it, though.'

Sean climbed easily enough at first for the ship was rolling only gently and besides, he was exhilarated at the thought that the torc was recovered, but the higher he climbed, the more difficult it became as the mast above him swayed sickeningly out over the sea before righting itself. He heard Annie cry out below him, but kept Mr Blundell's advice and was not tempted to look down. The rope was wet and slippery but rigid enough to make him feel secure. He climbed methodically hand after hand, foot after foot towards the top. The crow's nest was an empty water barrel, holed in the bottom and pulled to the top of the main mast, where it was secured with ropes. It was a temporary construction that the Captain had ordered so that a lookout might be kept for errant icebergs floating south. Sean knew the sailors dreaded their duties there and had heard them complaining bitterly of the cold suffered in a two-hour watch. He peered now over the edge of the barrel and looked down below him at the tiny people on the deck. Suddenly, and for the first time, his confidence left him and his knees weakened. He could see the Captain by the wheel, his telescope scouring the horizon, and the crowd of emigrants on the deck all looking up at him. He was tempted to wave down to them in defiance, but decided it might be too provocative. Annie, though, was waving up at him. He could not hear what she was shouting and he felt at that moment very alone and cold. But when a few minutes later he heard Fiddler Donnelly playing 'The Blackbird and the Hen', his favourite jig, and saw the passengers linking arms as they danced below him on the deck, he felt a surge of pride at their solidarity that sent shivers of warmth into his cold limbs.

The fine weather of the day was not to last. Sean saw it coming, a dark squall moving in across the sea from the west, covering the sun and darkening the world beneath. The wind came first, heralding the rain. Sean took what cover he could, crouching down in the barrel. He took his first sip of rum from Mr Blundell's flask. The taste was too sickly for him, but the feeling of nausea was at once replaced by a glow of shuddering warmth. It was, however, only a temporary respite, for as night came on he lost all feeling in his feet and hands.

The squall passed on into the darkness but the damage was done, for the sea now heaved with a deep swell that sent the crow's nest swinging clear out over the churning black sea below him. To look made Sean sick with fear, so he huddled in the bottom of the barrel and sang all the songs Fiddler Donnelly had taught him to play, over and over again. He recited the Holy Mass several times that long black night, not only out of fear for his life, but to make the time pass more quickly. He had always found that if he concentrated in church, the hour passed by less reluctantly. But with all the songs and masses sung and every jig and reel whistled through, there was little else to do but to reflect on his present sorry predicament. Only the knowledge that the torc was theirs once again prevented total gloom from setting in. He wondered where Mr Blundell could have hidden the torc and longed to see it again – all this discomfort would be worth while if he could only see it and touch it once more.

When he woke, he was stiff and numb. He had been woken not by the thunder of the waves – they had been his lullaby – but by a yolk-red light that had penetrated his eyelids. Peering out over the barrel he saw the entire sky which was lit in the east from end to end, blood-red at the centre and suffused with pink at the edges. He turned his face to the other horizon beyond the bow of the ship. Sean looked for a long time at the barely perceptible dark line on the western horizon. It was the only part of the ocean where cloud met the sea in a line still hazy from the night. It could be a layer of low cloud or simply an illusion. His mind was numb from cold and sleep but the longer he looked the more sure he became that he had sighted America. His excitement exploded.

'Land!' he bellowed, cupping his hands to the deserted decks below. 'Land! I see land! I see America!' And he went on shouting until he saw Mr Blundell emerging on to the deck, pulling on his coat, followed shortly after by the Captain who snatched Mr Blundell's telescope from him. Up from the steerage came the emigrants pouring on to the main deck, straining for the first glimpse of land; and sleepy-eyed and bemused came the cabin passengers wrapped in their shawls and gowns. 'I have it,' called the Captain triumphantly. 'I have it. A perfect landfall. As I live and breathe, a perfect landfall.'

CHAPTER 11

SEAN WATCHED MR BLUNDELL STRIDE ACROSS the deck to the Captain. There followed a long animated conversation, Mr Blundell gesticulating angrily up at the crow's nest. Sean stamped his feet but could feel nothing. He blew on his purple-cold hands, but found no sensation of warmth. I suppose I am alive, he thought. Maybe this is how the spirits feel as they float above the living world. Then he saw Mr Blundell make his way to the foot of the rigging and begin the long climb up towards him.

'We've been lucky, my boy,' Mr Blundell said as he joined Sean in the barrel. 'That sky over there may look pretty, but it's as vicious a sky as I've ever seen. I'd say we've but an hour or two before the storm hits us. You stay up here in a storm like that and that'll be the finish of you. So I had a little word with the Captain down there and persuaded him you'll be needed on the pumps when it comes. Doesn't like storms, does our Captain – terrified of 'em. So you'll be coming down with me. Had a good night, have you, my boy? Can you climb down d'you suppose?'

'Sure I can't feel a thing below my elbows and knees,' Sean said. 'So how will I know if I'm gripping hard enough to hold on?'

'You won't,' said Mr Blundell, 'so you'll come down on my back. It's the only way; just cling to me like a limpet, but don't throttle me else your sister will lose a brother and I shall lose a good ship's boy. Up you get and hang on tight now.'

The descent was perilous and slow. Mr Blundell was forced often to pause to regain his breath and to adjust his balance. Halfway down he stopped completely for a few minutes, hugging the ropes. 'D'you still have some of my rum left, boy?'

'Most of it,' said Sean, his legs wrapped around Mr Blundell, his head pressed on to his shoulder.

'Good,' said Mr Blundell. 'I shouldn't like to think

it was wasted. I'm too old for this, my boy, but I think we're going to make it.'

Annie was the first to greet him when they reached the deck, throwing her hands around his neck and squeezing the breath from his body. Fiddler it was who first held out his hand to Mr Blundell and shook it and many other passengers did the same in a spontaneous display of thanks. 'Mr Blundell,' the Captain roared. 'That thieving tinker is to be kept to his duties all day and all night. You're not to let him out of your sight. Bring him to me as soon as this weather is passed and we'll see how he feels about another night up aloft in the crow's nest.' And he turned and went below.

Mr Blundell's orders were clear and immediately obeyed. 'Haul in the mainsail. Batten down all hatches. We may have America in sight, but there'll be one hell of a storm before we reach her. I'll be calling for every able-bodied man when it strikes.' And quite suddenly, as he was speaking, the sea fell flat around them and the wind eased, slackening the sails above them. 'It's on its way,' Mr Blundell said, looking up. 'It won't be long now.'

'Where is it, Sean?' Annie whispered as soon as they were alone. 'Where's the torc? Where did you put it? Where is it, where did you put it?'

'I never stole it, Annie,' Sean said. 'Mr Blundell did and he's hiding it somewhere safe. Why did he do it for us, Fiddler?'

'Who knows?' said Fiddler Donnelly, 'but that's a good man if ever I saw one – knows right from wrong. There'll be a place in heaven for him when the time comes, I can tell you that. And talking of heaven, I've about as much faith in this ship as the Blessed Peter had on the Sea of Gallilee.' And suddenly he paused and spoke in deadly earnest, looking at the lowering sky behind him. 'If anything should ever happen to me, you're to keep my fiddle, Sean, and you're to play it, and Annie, you're to dance to it, for the rest of your lives. 'Tis an evil morning, right enough. I never saw such a wicked sky as that.'

'Don't say such things, Fiddler,' Annie said. 'We've been through one storm and it wasn't much, well, I didn't think it was much, anyway.'

'Annie's right, Fiddler,' said Sean, but he was worried by Fiddler's doom-laden tone, so he changed the subject. 'Can we trust Mr Blundell?' he said. 'Do you think he'll give us back the torc? He won't keep it for himself, will he?'

'He's a good man, Sean, I'm sure of it,' said Fiddler Donnelly, a tremor of a smile on his lips, and then he added. 'Never fear, children, you'll have your torc back, and soon. 'Tis your talisman, children. It will keep you safe. Like your mother told you, it'll keep you safe.'

The storm was late in coming. The coast clearly visible by the late afternoon and there was feverish excitement on deck as the land grew ever closer and closer. Hopes were high that the promised storm would not catch them and that they would make the safety of port first. But catch them it did, and when it struck, it struck with such speed and violence that several passengers were swept overboard before they could reach the safety of the lower deck. Fiddler had already taken Annie below and he was playing his heart out, for he felt deep inside him a premonition that he would not have the chance to play his fiddle again. Annie sat by him, curled up against him for warmth.

Sean, meanwhile, was already down in the hold with two of the sailors, pumping as hard as his tired body would allow him. Down there he could feel the terrible power of the water seeking with every wave to penetrate the hull. As fast as they pumped the water out, it returned again and with interest, so that within half an hour they knew there could be no stopping it. The timbers appeared to have opened their pores to the sea, for water was seeping in everywhere. But they pumped on until the water was above their waists and it was only then that Mr Blundell ordered them to abandon the pumps and come up.

The decks were low in the water now, with the debris of a breaking ship strewn everywhere. The topmast came down first with a yawning crash, crushing the handrail like matchwood and leaving the barrel that had served as the crow's nest trailing in the boiling seas off the starboard side. 'Not a good place to be,' Mr Blundell shouted to Sean beside him. 'Go to your sister, my boy, it's where you belong. The ship is lost, I tell you. We're a mile or two off the coast and we shall go on the rocks. There's nothing can stop her now. When she strikes, stay below until she's settled. You'll never survive in that sea, not if you can't swim, and you can't, can you?' Sean shook his head. 'Go now, my boy, and good luck.' Sean was about to ask the whereabouts of the torc, but Mr Blundell was gone.

For some time, Sean, Annie and Fiddler

Donnelly sat together with the other passengers, waiting for the ship to founder. Most prayed in silence. Others had only strength enough to restrain their terror, crying quietly to themselves. The ship was listing badly to starboard now, and Sean, knowing how deep the water must be in the hold, wondered time and again if the ship could right itself after each violent lurch to starboard. Both Sean and Fiddler Donnelly kept calm only because Annie was there beside them and they felt they must not allow their fear to show. But had they known it, that was unnecessary because of all of them, Annie was the least afraid. She still talked incessantly, quite convinced the storm would pass and they would be walking safely next morning in the streets of Boston.

So when the *Pelican* struck, Annie was the only one on board who was surprised. A splintering shudder tore the ship and she reared up on her beam-end like a terrified horse, and never came down. In the pandemonium that followed the three of them sat quite still, their arms around each other. 'Mr Blundell said to wait,' Sean kept shouting to make himself heard above the screaming. 'He said it was our only chance. We must stay here.' He tried to persuade others to stay, but no one paid him any heed. They fought each other like animals to reach the companionway. It was a mad, instinctive panic, a stampede. One young mother was struggling to marshal her young family up the companionway and on to the deck. If Fiddler Donnelly had spent any time away from Annie or Sean during the voyage it was with this young widow from Clonakilty. He had often shared their food with her, and he left them now quite suddenly to help her with her children. 'I'll be back shortly,' he told them. 'Don't move from where you are. And mind you look after my fiddle now.'

But he never came back. Annie wanted to go to find him, but Sean restrained her. They heard his voice above as the boats were lowered away, but they never saw him again. More than once during the night the ship yawned and settled on the rocks, battered as she was by thunderous seas. 'They've no hope up there,' said Sean. 'No hope at all. All storms must end and sometime even this one will end. If the ship doesn't break up, Annie, we've a chance.'

By the time the children ventured out on deck in the new light of morning, only their half of the ship was left. Not a soul was to be seen on board, and all around in the sea floated the flotsam of death. The ship, or what was left of her, was perched high on the teeth of a great black rock that ran like a giant's causeway on to a small beach of yellow sand. The sea heaved around the base of the rock, exhausted after its great exertion.

With Fiddler Donnelly's fiddle case under his arm, Sean led Annie carefully over the rocks. They went slowly, for the seaweed was slimy and treacherous. They waded shoulder-high through the rock pools, Sean holding the fiddle case above his head, and at last reached the safety of the beach. If any others had survived, they were nowhere to be seen. They could see only the footprints of birds on the sand. Sean called out again and again for Fiddler and for Mr Blundell, but only the gulls replied.

'Is this 'Merica?' Annie asked. 'Do you think it's really 'Merica?'

' 'Spose it must be,' said Sean.

'Why did Fiddler have to leave?' Annie said. 'Why does everyone we love have to leave us?'

They searched the rocks and the beaches for a mile in both directions but found only the washed-up fragments of the wreck. There were a few sodden clothes but no bodies.

'He left us his fiddle, Annie,' Sean said, opening

the black case and taking it out carefully. 'Said we should play it and dance to it, remember. And we will, and whenever we do, we'll remember him.' And he put it under his chin and picked up the bow. As he did so he heard something rattle inside the fiddle. He shook it to be sure his ears had not deceived him and then peered inside. The thin dawning sun caught a glint of gold that was quite unmistakable.

'What is it, Sean?' Annie asked.

''Tis the torc,' said Sean, sitting back on his haunches. ''Tis the golden torc. The two of them did it for us, Annie, Fiddler and Mr Blundell both, and we shall never be able to thank them.'

'God will. He'll be thanking them right now, and so will Mother,' said Annie, and then, 'Sean, I'm that hungry, I could eat a horse, honest I could.'

'Then let's find one,' said Sean, and they walked up the beach and into America.

CHAPTER 12

AMERICA, ANNIE DECIDED, WAS QUITE DIFFERENT from Ireland. More trees grew here than she had ever seen in her life before, and they were great tall trees, not bent and stunted by the wind. The leaves shone scarlet and gold in the thin morning light, falling like flakes of sun around them.

They were reluctant at first to plunge into the trees and kept to the high-water mark along the beach. Time and again they called out for Fiddler and Mr Blundell, but there was no sign of life. They came at last upon a track that took them through the woods following the path of a broad, sandy creek. The carpet of fallen leaves cushioned their bare feet, and weak as they were they ran now from tree to tree, racing each other through the leaves, Annie always ahead because Sean was encumbered with the fiddle case. When he stopped suddenly, Annie taunted him at first.

'Have you had enough, Sean?' she cried, puffing and blowing in her triumph.

'I trod on something,' said Sean, and he bent down and brushed the leaves away. 'Look, Annie, nuts – sure there's hundreds of them.' What kind of nuts they were they neither knew nor cared, but sat down side by side by the squirrel's horde in a silent nut-feast that did not stop until both could eat no more. Replete, they lay back in the leaves.

'D'you think we're the only ones left?' said Annie, closing her eyes against the glare of the sun as it filtered through the trees above her.

'Seems like it,' Sean said. Both of them were so exhilarated by their own survival that they found it difficult to mourn their fellow passengers. The immensity of the tragedy was not apparent to them. Only the loss of Fiddler Donnelly over-shadowed their relief and joy.

Annie sat up suddenly. 'Listen,' she whispered. 'Did you hear that?' Close behind them came the rustling of feet moving through the leaves. The two children sat like statues, hardly daring to breathe as the halting, shuffling gait came closer. It was Annie who called out, 'It's only us. Annie and Sean O'Brien. Who's there?' But there was no reply and all the while the rustling came ever closer. She called out again, 'We're from the ship, just like you. Who are you?' Sean tried to hold her back, but Annie broke away from his arm, sprang to her feet and ran out to the open, shouting, 'It's only us, it's only us.' Sean stayed hidden where he was and was amazed when he saw Annie suddenly double up with laughter, pointing into the trees and clearly quite unable to contain herself. ''Tis a pig, 'tis a 'Merican pig and it looks just like an Irish pig, maybe a bit cleaner. Come see, Sean, come see.' The pig paid them no attention, absorbed as she was in her own search for nuts, her snout pushing aside the leaves like a plough, munching as she came.

'That is a farm sow,' said Sean, 'and that means that she's out on the wander and she'll go home. If we follow her, she'll lead us to a village or farm. They must have farms here like at home – Father said they did.'

Sure enough, after a day's patient vigil following

the pig in circles around the woods, she lifted her snout from the ground at last and made off home. Once or twice she had cast her mean little eyes on the children warning them not to come too close, and they sensibly obliged, keeping their distance as they followed her. As the pig neared home she broke into a gentle trot, her great ears slapping on her neck.

Home proved to be a cluster of wooden houses built around the end of a creek. A few small fishing boats were drawn up on the sand, and the woodland around had been cleared away to fields behind the houses. The children stayed in the shelter of the trees and watched the pig as she squeezed under a fence and out into a grassy field beyond, where a number of other pigs were grazing. She joined them and became one of them.

Annie was all for marching straight up to a house and hammering on the door, but Sean was more cautious. 'How do we know they'll be friendly?' he asked. 'Maybe they'll set their dogs on us. Sure there's dogs everywhere.' And in the end it was one of these dogs that decided the issue. A rangy-looking foxhound came lumbering up the track towards them, sniffed the air and set up a high-pitched yowling that brought every dog in the village running in a pack. Geese and hens scattered in terror, and Sean and Annie too were tempted to run for it, but they both knew that was pointless and so stood their ground as the dogs surrounded them. With a circle of enraged dogs gambolling around them, the children linked arms and moved slowly down the track towards the houses to meet the group of villagers who were advancing towards them, every one of them, it seemed, carrying a gun. Children who ventured out of the houses were dragged back inside and the doors slammed. The dogs were called off and fell silent.

'Is this Boston, 'Merica?' Annie asked. 'We're looking for Boston, 'Merica.' One person laughed and then another and another, until Annie found herself the only one not laughing, and was forced to join in.

'Hell, no,' said one of the ladies, leaning on her gun. 'This ain't Boston. Boston's a mite bigger'n this.' And they all laughed again. 'You gone and got yourselves lost out in them woods, I guess,' she went on. 'Why, you ain't no more'n little children! What's your ma and pa doing lettin' you run wild out in them woods? Where you from anyhow? You ain't from hereabouts.'

'Ireland,' Sean said. 'We come from Ireland. And the ship we were on went on the rocks last night in the storm. We've been looking for our friends. You've not seen anyone else come this way p'raps?'

In an instant, the smiles vanished and the villagers began to back away from them. 'Ireland? You on one of them migrant ships?' the lady said, her gun held up now in front of her. Sean nodded. 'Did you have the sickness on board?'

'Some of them died,' said Annie, ''cos there wasn't much food, and the water was bad, terrible bad.'

'I knew it,' the lady said, backing away and taking the crowd with her.

'A plague ship,' someone muttered. 'They're from a plague ship.'

'You keep your distance, d'you hear? Don't come any closer, not if you've a mind to go on livin'.' And the lady's gun was up now, cocked and pointed at them.

'I don't understand it. What's the matter with you?' Sean asked, perplexed at the change of mood. 'Why are you all looking at us like that?'

' 'Cos you got the plague, son, that's why,' said an angry voice from the back of the crowd. 'Every ship that comes into Boston from Ireland is full of it. I heard tell there's folk dying in the streets of Boston and all because of your Irish plague. Heard tell there's whole families wiped out with it.'

'But they didn't die of the plague on the ship,' said Annie vehemently, and she stepped forward. ' 'Twas the water and the food, like I told you.'

'Git back, little girl, else I'll shoot, and that's a promise,' said the lady, pulling her gun up to her shoulder. 'We cain't take no risks. There's a hundred folk here in this village and all of us is in mortal danger long as you stay here. Now you just pass on by and you'll come to no harm.'

'But we need water,' said Sean. 'Won't you give us some water? 'Tis all we want.' The villagers spoke amongst themselves, looking over their shoulders from time to time at the two children.

'You got any kin-folk, any family?' said the same lady who seemed to speak for all of them. She wore a bonnet of russet brown, had a very red face underneath it and very few teeth.

'Of course we have,' said Annie defensively. 'We've come to 'Merica to look for our father. P'raps you've seen him, have you? He's the biggest man you've ever seen, higher'n any of you and he has a red beard with white bits in it and he came to Boston more'n a year ago. You've not seen him, have you? You could not mistake him, not in a million years. Patrick O'Brien he's called and he's my father.'

Her words seemed to disarm them instantly and smiles broke through suspicion and fear. They conferred once again. 'Mother always said 'twas terrible rude to whisper in company,' Annie announced loudly.

'Could you tell us how far it is to Boston?' Sean asked, trying to keep Annie from being any more offensive.

'Twelve, fifteen miles if you keep to the coast road,' said the lady in the bonnet. 'But we're thinking it would not be right to have you walking all the way to Boston and that on an empty stomach, not with night coming on, and winter in the air. Hell, no, it wouldn't be Christian. So here's what we're gonna do. Thar's a barn far side of town. Marty here will take you – he's my man. You kin spend the night thar and we'll bring you what you need and tomorrow first light you kin go in with the fish wagon into Boston. Marty will take you. But if we do this, thar's got to be a Holy Bible promise you'll stay inside that barn and come near no one, Holy Bible, you hear now?'

The barn was filled to the roof with the summer's hay, and sweeter than any Annie or Sean had ever smelt. There was until dark a regular procession of visitors bringing them all manner of food: sweet pies, fruit and bread. It was all left in baskets outside the door. 'Be quick and fetch it, now,' someone called. 'Less'n you want the dogs to have it.' They did not have to be asked twice. They ate more that evening sitting in the hay than they had eaten for the entire month before. The hot coffee was bitter and strange to them, but it warmed them through and through. Blankets were brought up for them as dusk fell, and a change of warm clothes and a pair of leather boots each.

'Sleep tight now, y'hear?' The voice was that of the lady in the bonnet. 'Marty will be by in the morning.'

Sean and Annie used the last of the light to dress in their new clothes. Everything was too big, but there were no holes and the cloth was warm and dry. They had the most difficulty with the boots for neither had ever in their lives worn shoes of any kind, and they stamped in delight up and down the earth floor of the barn for half an hour or more until they could walk in them without stumbling. Their squeals of laughter found an echo outside the barn door and closer investigation found an eye-ball in every crack in the timber. So Sean took out Fiddler's violin and began to play; and Annie lifted her woollen skirt above her boots and danced until the clapping came from outside and at last the scuffling sound of dancing feet. It was, thought Sean as he played, the only way they could thank these people for their kindness. When the darkness deepened and the children outside were shepherded away home, Sean and Annie climbed under the heavy blanket and curled up beside each other in the hay. Neither spoke. There was no need, for both were filled with a deep sense of contentment that wiped away all the wretched memories of the past.

CHAPTER 13

THE KNOCK CAME LOUD AND INSISTENT ON THE barn door and they woke out of a deep and untroubled sleep. Sean locked up the black fiddle case, shook it gently to hear the rattle of the torc, tucked it under his arm and unlatched the door. Outside was not just Marty and the fish wagon, but the entire population of the village it seemed was gathered at a discreet distance and clapping as they emerged from the barn.

'Where'd you learn to play and dance like that?' asked the lady in the russet-brown bonnet.

'We had a friend,' said Annie, 'did we not, Sean? He taught us but he's dead now, so we'll be doing his playing for him from now on.'

'Thank you, Ma'am,' Sean said quietly. 'You've been terrible kind to us.'

'Christian duty,' said the lady. 'Nearly forgot it though, didn't we? Just our Christian duty. Now you take good care in Boston. 'S'a wicked town for young folk like you to be 'lone in. Marty will see you get there safely. You'd best sit up in the back with the fish. You'll smell a bit at the end of it, but what's the harm in that? Thar's worser smells than fresh fish. On your way, Marty. And make sure you get back afore dark. Good luck little people. God go with you.'

And so, sitting amongst baskets of fish, the two children rode away towards Boston with Marty chewing and spitting his tobacco further than Sean had ever seen anyone spit before. 'Thar's an art to it,' he said. 'Why, I kin knock a hairy-legged buzzard clean off his post at fifty paces. Don't kill him of course, but he hears it a-coming and he knows it's one of mine so he don't wait around, no sir.'

At first Sean declined the offer of tobacco from Marty, but Annie was not to be out-faced and chewed on the leathery mixture until her jaws ached. 'Got to use your tongue like a catapult, little girl,' said Marty. 'You curls your tongue around, you throws up your head and away she goes.' Annie's first attempt barely cleared the side of the wagon, and Marty shook his head and offered her some more tobacco. Sean could resist it no longer, and soon both of them were chewing and spitting together so that the road behind them was liberally marked with their efforts. By the time they reached Boston both children felt more than a little sick and Marty could still spit three times as far as their best attempts. He dropped them in the city centre at mid-morning, pressed half a dollar into Sean's hand, ruffled their hair in farewell and was gone.

Boston was a teeming city of refugees. Children were out begging at every street corner, the doorways and steps of the great buildings were strewn with poor gaunt wretches who stared at the two children as they passed by. Of course, the sight of such misery was not new to them, but it was on such a vast scale and so unexpected. Had not their father written of a paradise on earth? Was not America a land of plenty? It was as if the whole Irish nation had dumped itself destitute on the streets of Boston. The sheer size of the place with its tall buildings and wide streets bewildered them, for until this moment no place was ever bigger or grander than Cork. Numbed by the bustle and the noise, they walked the streets in a daze hand in hand.

'Hamilton Street,' said Sean suddenly. 'We have to find Hamilton Street. That's where Father's letter came from. Mother said we might find news of him there.'

'Have you ever seen so many people?' said Annie. 'Sure 'tis like an anthill.' They thought first to ask directions from the more respectable people, thinking they would know better which street was which, but these ignored them, turning their heads and often covering their mouths before hurrying away. One gentleman even used his cane on them, shooing them away like dogs.

On turning into Washington Square, Annie tugged violently at Sean's arm, almost making him drop the fiddle case. 'Did you ever see such a thing?' she said. 'He's black, black as night all over.'

'What is, Annie?'

'That man holding the horse. Have you ever seen the like of it, Sean?'

'Stop your staring, Annie,' said Sean.

'Well he's looking at us 's'if we were something strange, so I'll go right on looking at him. Better'n that, I'll ask him if he knows Hamilton Street. D'you think he speaks like we do, Sean? I mean, will he understand what I say?' She crossed the road and marched right up to him. 'Can you speak English, Sir?' she asked.

'Some,' said the man, looking down at Sean and Annie. 'I been speakin' it all my life, lil' missy.'

'Then can you be telling me where Hamilton Street is?' Annie asked. 'We're looking for our father and he was there some while back, maybe a year ago.'

'Well, lil' missy, if he were there that long ago, he sure ain't likely to be there now. They dies like flies down there. Why, there's so many folk livin' down there there ain't air enough for 'em to breathe. If he got any sense he'll be long gone by now. 'Tain't far to go, lil' missy, but you take my advice and don't go livin' in no house in Hamilton Street.' And he told them the way, but Annie could not take her eyes off the man's shining black face, so she soon lost track of his directions. Fortunately Sean was listening more carefully.

'How come you got so black, Mister?' Annie asked suddenly.

'Well, lil' missy, I puts it on every morning before sun-up and I takes it off every night. You rub me hard enough an' it'll come off just like the brown off a hen's egg. Wanna try, lil' missy?' And he held out his forearm. Annie wet her forefinger and rubbed until it was dry, but it seemed to make no impression. 'Well, bless my soul, looks as if I put it on once too often,' said the black man, his great white eyes wide with panic. 'Wind must have changed direction and I'm stuck with it for life. Let that be a lesson to you, lil' missy.' Annie caught the mocking tone in his voice and saw the smile in his teasing eyes and began at last to understand.

'Are you telling me you're born like that?' she asked, still not quite believing it.

'That's what my mammy said, lil' missy. You mean you ain't never seen no black man before? Where you bin all your life, lil' missy? You from Ireland? Town's full of them Irish folk – most of 'em sick. Ain't they got no black men out in Ireland? We got all sorts here in 'Merica. Yes sir, there's folk from all over – England, Germany, Dutchland, Ireland, Swedenland – there's hundreds of 'em comin' in every day, 'cos this is a mighty big country an' there's room for everyone who's a mind to come. Yes, sir, mighty big country an' there's room for everyone who's a mind to come. Yes, sir, mighty big. You play that fiddle of yours?'

'A bit,' said Sean, 'a bit.'

'That's fine, boy, fine, but you'd best keep a tight hold on it. There's folk about here who'd have the clothes off your back. Take care now, d'you hear? Take care.'

Annie wanted to stay talking but Sean led her away, hugging the fiddle case close to him. She was still looking over her shoulder and muttering on about the black man when they turned the corner into Hamilton Street. Like all the streets they had walked through to get there, the houses were several stories high and colonised rather than lived in. There were people at every window and door. Their shacks spilled out on to the pavements and into the gardens, clinging like unsightly limpets to the ground floor of every house. At each door Sean stopped and asked after his father, but they either laughed at him or shook their heads sadly. Most had only been there it seemed a few months and those that had lived there longer and could have remembered him, did not.

CHAPTER 14

THEY WERE GOING UP THE STEPS INTO THE VERY last house in the street when they were confronted with a small, round-faced man in a blue velvet jacket. He wore a red handkerchief around his neck and high, shining boots and was followed by a tall greyhound of a man who looked at them greedily.

'Have you just got in from the old country?' he said with a smile that was too broad to be believed in. 'And I suppose you'll be looking for somewhere to sleep? Well you've come to the right place. I've a little attic room, just suit you fine it would. Two dollars a week – isn't that a bargain now? All right, I'm a fair man. You're down on your luck, I can see that. A dollar and a half, how will that be?'

'We're not looking for somewhere to stay,' said Sean, but the man ignored him.

'What about the fiddle?' said the man advancing down the step towards them. 'Now that fiddle must be worth a fair bit. I'll take it off you and you have the room free for a month.'

''Tis not mine to sell,' said Sean, gripping the fiddle case tightly and backing down the steps on to the street.

'Then I'll just be borrowing it for a while,' said the man, the smile gone suddenly from his face. At that moment the children sensed the threat in his voice and turned to escape. But their way was barred by a line of ragged children behind them. Sean did not hesitate, but went through them like a bull, head down and charging, dragging Annie along behind him. Fear drove them on in their flight until a look over his shoulder told Sean that they had thrown off their pursuers, all, that is, except the tall greyhound of a man who still loped after them, his long strides bringing him closer all the while. Sean knew that Annie was tiring now as they turned the corner into Washington Square once more. There seemed nowhere to run to, nowhere to hide and Sean could feel the man behind him now without having to look. Whether it was wet leaves or a slippery paving stone Sean never knew, but his legs were gone from under him suddenly and the fiddle case was thrown out of his hands by the force of his fall. When he looked up he saw the tall man coming for him only a few yards away. Annie had recovered the fiddle case and was shouting for him to run, but Sean knew it was no good. He leaped to his feet to face his attacker, but quite unaccountably the man had come to a halt and was backing away.

'You after somethin' friend?' came a deep voice from behind him. Sean turned to see the black man they had met before, his arm around Annie. ' 'Cos if you are, you gotta remember that these is my friends, an if they don't like you then I don't either. Get my meanin', friend?' Clearly he did, for the man had vanished by the time Sean looked back again. 'Now you two is gonna get into all kinds of trouble, I can see that. I's can see I's gonna have to keep my eye on you two. Take my advice, an' keep to the city centre – people is more 'spectable there. Hope that fiddle of yours ain't broke, boy.' Sean took the case from Annie and opened it up. He took the fiddle out and examined it closely. Nothing was broken.

'That there is a fine fiddle, boy – rattles some, somethin' loose inside maybe, but looks good as new to me.'

'Thank you, Mister,' said Sean, closing the case quickly.

'Don't thank me, boy,' said the black man, walking slowly back to his horses and stroking their noses. 'Just don't like folk frightening my horses here – 'sides, he looked mighty unfriendly that fellow.'

'I'm Annie, and my brother's called Sean.'

'An' I'm Lil' Luke, Miss Annie. An' it's been my privilege, my privilege.' And he raised his hat and bowed to them.

'Little Luke?' said Annie. 'But you're not little.'

'I was when I began, lil' missy. An' that's when my mammy first knew me, so I guess that's why she called me Lil' Luke, an' it kind of stuck.' At that moment the door of the house by which they were standing opened and two grey-haired ladies in fine dresses emerged and entered the carriage.

'Home, Little Luke,' one of them said. 'We'll be late for tea, and you know I never like to be late for tea.'

'No, Ma'am,' said Little Luke, and he winked at the children who stood to one side as Little Luke whipped up the horses and drove away out of sight, but not without a last lifting of his hat in farewell.

That night it was cold in Boston, bitterly cold. They spent Marty's half-dollar on some warm soup and a loaf of bread and then set out to find some shelter from the cold. But there was none to be found. And so it was that they slept their first night in Boston out on the streets, curled up side by side under Will's cloak on the pavement.

One night of such intense cold was enough to force Sean to collect his thoughts. Without food and shelter he knew they would perish. They had only a few cents left and there was only one way, short of stealing, that they could find the money to live. They would have to beg for it, just as others were doing.

'I won't beg,' said Annie, cuddled tight into his back and trying to forget the cold of the pavement. 'I won't do it, I won't.'

''Tis not exactly begging I have in mind,' Sean said.

'Could we not sell the torc, Sean?'

'I'd starve first,' said Sean. 'All that time at home Mother could have sold it for food, could she not? I asked her to often enough. She told me then, "Sean," she said, "there are some things, Sean, more important than living." That's what she said, Annie, and you heard her – you were there. 'Twas just before little Joe passed away.'

'I've been thinking a lot about Mother, Sean,' Annie said. 'She'll be dead by now, won't she? 'Tis strange not to know if your Mother is live or dead.'

''Tis best not to think on it. Don't speak of her, Annie. It makes me think of her and I don't want to, I don't want to ever again. She's dead and we have to live, Annie, that's all that matters now. We have to find Father and we have to bring him the torc as we promised Mother we would. And that's why tomorrow I'm going to stand on this street corner and play my fiddle and you're going to dance, Annie, as you've never danced before; and they'll throw enough money into our fiddle case as they pass by, enough to keep us in food and enough to pay the rent on some little room somewhere 'til we can find out where Father's gone. Now that's not begging, is it Annie? That's working for a living.'

'And Fiddler would be happy,' Annie said. 'Would he not?'

'Maybe he is,' said Sean, 'and if he's looking down on us tomorrow I hope we can make him proud of us. My fingers are so cold, Annie that I wonder if

I'll ever be able to work them properly.'

'Then I'll blow on them,' Annie said. 'Just like I did with Fiddler.'

So that winter the two children stood on their corner by the City Hall and played and danced to the people as they came and went. And the coins fell often enough into the fiddle case beside them to provide them with a roof over their heads, a crude, damp basement they shared with a dozen other wretched migrants and innumerable squealing rats. But the days out in the cold and the driving rain and snow were beginning to take their toll. Their spirits began to fade and the cold gnawed at their bones and sapped their health. Annie could dance now for only short periods before her legs weakened and she had to sit by Sean's feet to regain her breath and summon up the strength to go on. She kept cheerful and talkative, but the life was beginning to go out of her; and Sean, wracked by a terrible cough that would not leave him, was too weak himself to notice it in her.

More than once they saw Little Luke riding high on his carriage in his great brown cloak and derby hat, and he always waved as he passed by and lifted his hat. Sometimes he would stop on the other side of the street and Annie would leave her dancing and run across to see him. These meetings seemed to brighten her and afterwards she would chatter happily to Sean about how good it was to have a friend like Little Luke.

One grey November morning the carriage stopped in the road opposite them and the two grey-haired ladies they had seen before peered out of the window at the two children. Sean was too busy playing to notice them, but Annie told Sean to play his heart out, and then threw up her chin and danced as she had never danced before, until Little Luke whipped up the horses and drove on.

When the snows came before Christmas, they scraped away the snow from their pavement and played and danced on; and the people still came to listen to their music, clapping and cheering after each dance. Their applause warmed her heart and kept her feet pointing as Fiddler Donnelly had taught her. It was on Christmas Eve itself that she collapsed as she danced, and when Sean lifted her up out of the snow to cradle her in his arms, he could find no signs of life left in her.

CHAPTER 15

THE CROWD THAT GATHERED WAS IN TWO MINDS. Every one of them knew what they should do, but rumours of the plague were more rife than the plague itself and made them hesitate. There was talk of calling for a doctor, but no one dared come too close. Sean was oblivious to them. He kept calling to Annie to wake up, but she lay limp in his arms and no amount of shaking could awaken her.

A shining stick of ebony came waving its way through the crowd, and behind it came a voice so imperious and sharp that the crowd parted instantly and meekly. The elderly lady who owned the voice was dressed all in dark blue from her fur-lined bonnet to her boots, and behind her came another lady whose face was the image of the first but who was dressed entirely in forest green, and behind her came the giant figure of Little Luke in his cloak and his derby hat.

'Stand aside,' called the lady in blue. 'Stand aside this instant.' And she looked down at the two children on the pavement and turned to the crowd. 'We should be ashamed to see such a sight on our city streets. Christmas Eve is it not? And was there not another child somewhere else who could find no shelter on just such an evening? Dear God, are we nothing but innkeepers that we stand gaping and do nothing? Little Luke,' she went on, pointing her stick down at Annie, 'pick up that child and bring her to my carriage this instant.'

'But Ma'am,' said one of the gentlemen in the crowd, raising his hat, 'the child could be dying of the plague. You can see they are off one of those immigrant ships, and there's not one of them that doesn't bring the plague with them.'

'Sir,' said the lady in blue, fixing the unfortunate man with a penetrating glare. 'Tell me, Sir, are you a doctor?'

'No, Ma'am.'

'Then, Sir, you have no right to make a medical judgement on the matter, have you?'

'No, Ma'am.'

'Quite so. And even if the child had been touched by the plague, every member of my family has lived out their full three-score years and ten – that's quite sufficient for anyone, one must not be greedy, Sir – and I shall do the same, plague or no plague. To the carriage, Little Luke. And Martha,' she said to the lady in forest green, 'you'd better bring that wretched little boy with you. I have never liked boys, Martha, as you know – such unnecessary creatures I find – but if we take the one I suppose we must take the other.'

Sean barely had time to pack away his fiddle before being led away by the hand towards the carriage. Once inside he sat down opposite the two ladies and put his arm around Annie, who was covered up to her chin by a fur rug and a white shawl. 'My sister, is she dead?' he asked.

'Not at all, not at all. Stuff and nonsense,' said the lady in blue. 'Drive on, Little Luke, drive on. As soon as we get some warm food into her, and tuck her up in a nice warm bed, she'll be right as rain, won't she, Martha?' And Martha nodded, smiling shyly at Sean from under her bonnet.

Sean looked from one to the other in amazement, for each possessed a thin pointed nose, bright deep-set eyes, a proud jutting chin over a long and elegant neck. Even the lines about their eyes and mouths seemed to be the same length, angle and depth. It was quite impossible to tell them apart. 'Have you stared long enough, young man?' said the lady in blue. 'And if you are about to make excuses, do not. Boys are all the same. They have no manners, none at all, isn't that right, Martha?' And Martha nodded again but her smile was more open now and Sean knew she did not agree. 'You'll perhaps have noticed from your rude observations that Martha and I are somewhat alike. That is hardly surprising since we are twin sisters. So as not to confuse people, I always dress in blue, dark blue, and Martha always dresses in green. I am known to everyone as Miss Henry, and she as Miss Martha, is that clear, young man?'

'Yes, Ma'am,' said Sean, and quite suddenly Annie stirred beside him and sat up, looking around her.

'God's will it was,' said Miss Henry, leaning forward. 'God's will we were passing this way, that we came in time to save you, child,' and she paused for a moment, puzzled, then turned to Martha. 'Martha, why were we passing this way? When I come to think of it, and I am thinking of it, why has Little Luke been insisting on driving us this way? It is quite the wrong way home from the store, quite the wrong way. And have you noticed, Martha, for I have, that he has contrived to stop by the City Hall steps several times, has he not? Twice last week a horse went lame in the very same spot, and not a month ago the wheel, you remember, was about to fall off in that very same place. And was it not then that Little Luke first pointed out these two unfortunate children? And was it not Little Luke who drew our attention to the crowd this very afternoon? And was it not he who suggested I might want to step down to investigate?' and she sat bolt upright in her seat, her face taut with fury. 'Martha, I declare we've been duped, bamboozled, led by our noses, Martha.' And then she tapped the carriage roof with her stick and in a shrill voice cried, 'Luke, Luke. Stop the carriage this instant.'

The carriage rocked to a standstill and Little Luke appeared at the window, smiling broadly under his brown derby. 'Somethin' the matter, Miss Henry?'

'Indeed there is, Luke. Indeed there is. Are you a bamboozler, Luke?'

'Yes'm,' said Little Luke, still smiling. 'If you say so, Ma'am. Is that all?'

'Positively evil, Luke, positively evil. Martha, I think this man is a trickster and a charlatan. Do you not remember his daily sonorous appeals at the breakfast table about the poor little immigrant Irish children starving on the streets of Boston? And this very morning at breakfast, Martha, was it not he who talked of the homeless child of Bethlehem?' But she paused once more and her face suddenly took on the look of an agitated hen. 'No, Martha,' she said slowly, 'it was not Little Luke, it was you who said that, was it not? There has been a conspiracy against me. Martha, you have betrayed me.'

Annie glanced quickly across at Little Luke and the look that passed between them was evidence enough to confirm Miss Henry's suspicions. 'I thought as much,' she said, nodding her head. 'I thought as much. A plot, a plot, an iniquitous plot to dupe an old lady. I see it all now. Soften the old girl up first, was that it? Then drive her back and forth each day so she can catch a glimpse of them, eh? Then arrange a simulated swoon just as we passed by. I see it all now, I see it all.'

All this while Sean was trying with difficulty to grasp the implications of what the lady in blue was saying. He could see from the triumphant grin on Little Luke's face that there had indeed been a conspiracy and he was about to turn to Annie when he found Miss Henry's stick against his chest pinning him back into his seat. 'Boys! Boys! Is there nothing they would not descend to? I can presume, can I not, young man, that you are indeed one of the conspirators? You are a rogue, sir, a rascal.' Sean shook his head quite unable to speak. 'No? Come now, am I to believe that the look of bewilderment on your dirty face is an honest look, eh? Is there no end to your shamming?'

'He did not know, Ma'am,' Annie said, laying her hand on the stick. 'I never told him a thing about it. 'Twas just Little Luke and me, we planned it all alone. Sure he's a shocking bad liar is my brother, no good at it at all, never has been, so I never said a word to him, not a word. And that's the honest truth of it. And Little Luke, Ma'am, he did it for us because he felt sorry for us, so don't be angry with him, Ma'am.' And she took Sean's hand. 'Open the door, Little Luke,' she said, 'and let us out. Did I not tell you it wouldn't work? We'll not go where we're not wanted. We're not beggars, and we'll not be starting now.'

'Sit still,' said Miss Henry, pushing Annie back with her stick. 'I say who climbs aboard my carriage and I say who leaves it.' And she turned to Miss Martha who was smiling broadly. 'I need only one more explanation, Martha. Why did you not ask me directly? Why did you not tell me you wanted to take these two in? We've never had secrets from each other before, Martha. I'm hurt that you felt you had to deceive me into this.'

'Henry,' said Miss Martha, her voice so soft and gentle that Annie and Sean had to strain to hear it. 'I would have asked you directly, and I was going to, but do you remember when we first saw those poor hungry wretches from Ireland pouring off the ships in the spring? I said to you then that we should perhaps try to help them if we could. And you told me there were too many of them, that the problem was too big, that to choose one or two would be to deny the others. Do you remember, Henry? So when Little Luke came to me with his story of these two poor dear children, I dared not tell you about it for fear you would refuse. Do you see? And what was worse, one of them was a little boy, and we all know what you feel about little boys.'

Miss Henry sat in silence for a few moments, her eyes lowered. 'It is true that most little boys are horrid and unnecessary,' she said, looking deliberately at Sean. 'But this, I surmise, is a fine little boy, of noble character, for he does not deceive like his sister. Such people are rare and I like them whether they be boys or girls. You may come and sit beside me, young man. And Martha, you may sit beside your fellow conspirator. And as for you, Little Luke,' she said, pointing her stick at Little Luke's throat, 'you will drive us all home as fast as you can. My little friends here have need of a hot bath and a change of clothes. Don't stand there grinning, Little Luke. Strike up those horses this instant.'

'Yes'm, right away, Miss Henry,' said Little Luke, and winking at Annie he went on. 'See, missy, I told lil' you she had a heart of gold, pure gold.'

'Luke!'

'I'm goin', Miss Henry, I'm goin'.'

'Miss Henry,' said Annie as they clattered over the top bridge and away from the city. 'Miss Henry, why do they call you Miss Henry? Henry is a name for boys, is it not?'

'Mostly,' said Miss Henry. 'But this Henry is a lady and always has been since the beginning when my dear departed mother saw that my sister Martha and I were a little bit difficult to tell apart. So she decided to keep my hair cut short and call me Henry, and leave Martha's long and call her Martha. That suited just fine until Martha and I both started wearing hats. But the name stuck. Only family call me Miss Henry, isn't that right Martha?'

'I guess Sean and Annie are family now, aren't they, Henry?' Martha said.

'I guess they are at that,' Miss Henry said, looking down her nose at Sean, and for the first time her face cracked into a smile that set them all laughing.

CHAPTER 16

HOME WAS A GREAT GABLED, RED-BRICK mansion bristling with smoking chimneys high up on Beacon Hill above Boston. The house itself was hidden behind a great wall that was shrouded in rustling ivy. Annie was full of questions all the way. 'Why is it you need more than one chimney, Miss Henry?' she asked, peering out of her window.

'Questions, questions, child,' tutted Miss Henry. 'Well, perhaps one would be lonely,' she said in exasperation.

'Father built the tallest chimney in all Ireland,' Annie said. 'But it was never as tall as those.'

'You have a father then?' said Miss Martha.

'To be sure we have,' said Annie. 'He's in 'Merica somewhere. We've looked for him everywhere, but we cannot even find anyone who remembers him can we, Sean?'

'And your mother?' Miss Henry asked.

'She's dead,' said Sean quickly, and Annie looked across at him, her eyes filling with tears.

'Yes, she's dead,' she said, and she fell silent until they stood inside the great hall of the mansion. Above them hung a glittering crystal chandelier lit with innumerable flickering candles. The children stood beneath it looking up, mouths gaping.

'Miss Henry, 's'almost dark and you' late again, always late. An' what's that you brung in?' Bustling down the stairs came a large black lady whose round face furrowed with indignation. 'Miss Henry,' she said, examining Sean and Annie critically from a distance. 'I don' know where you got 'em from, but they's goin' back. This house is jus' big enough for the four of us an' sometimes a might too small even then. An' Luke, you wipe your feet before you bring that snow in here all over my floor.'

'Little Luke,' said Miss Henry, 'then you never even told Bessie, you never even told your own wife?'

'Told me what 'zactly?' said Bessie, eyeing Little Luke with great suspicion. 'That man o' mine, he never tells me nothin' 'portant. Why, I even had to tell him to marry me 'cos he forgot himself.'

'I have to reveal to you a most terrible conspiracy, Bessie,' said Miss Henry. 'A conspiracy hatched up between my wicked sister and your bamboozler of a husband and that green-eyed little girl there – they conspired together to blackmail me into taking in these unfortunate children. But for the sake of this most excellent little boy and because I am a most forgiving creature, these two children are most welcome to stay here for the time being. See if you can find them some respectable clothing. They must be bathed at once, Bessie. I want them brought down to dinner pink and new and smelling like daisies.'

It was the first hot bath either of the children could remember and Annie was reluctant both to undress and then to step into the tub by the fire; but Bessie was most insistent and anyway Annie was somewhat intrigued by the possibility of sitting down in hot water. She had bathed in the river of course in the summer back in Ireland, but this was new to her and, as she soon discovered, something to be savoured. By the end of her bath, she and Bessie had become firm allies against the world and already the best of friends.

In another bathroom down the corridor, Little Luke scrubbed Sean till his skin tingled. 'If we don't get it right now,' he said, 'Miss Henry'll send us right back to do it again. She's a fine woman, Master Sean, but stubborn as a mule.'

Sean was deep in thought as he lay back with the water lapping under his chin. 'D'you know something, Little Luke,' he said. 'That was the first secret my sister has ever kept from me – or maybe it wasn't. I thought she was dead, honest I did. I can't make up my mind whether I should be angry with her or not.'

'She'd make a fine actress, Miss Annie would,' Little Luke said. 'Now bend your head so I kin scrub your neck.'

'Why did you do it, Little Luke? I mean, why did you choose us?'

' 'Cos I likes you, Master Sean. 'Cos no one's ever tried to rub the black off my skin afore, 'cos each time I passed by, your fiddlin' an' her dancin' made me happy with the world, an' 'cos you had the blackest neck I ever did see. I was gonna get that neck clean or die in the 'tempt. Why, there's so much dirt behind here that you could grow a whole field of potatoes, an' I'm gonna git it all off.'

Miss Henry and Miss Martha looked on, horrified, at the dinner table that evening as the two children attacked the food. Knives and forks and spoons, it appeared, were quite superfluous to their needs, and the napkins stayed untouched and neatly folded on the polished mahogany table. After dinner was over, attempts were made to provide them with separate rooms, but neither would hear of it; and try as they did, Little Luke and Bessie were quite unable to persuade them to climb up into the bed to sleep. 'I will not sleep up in the air,' Annie had said. 'I have only to roll over and I'd be falling out of it.'

And they noticed too that everywhere Sean went, the fiddle case went too. It stayed beside him all through dinner and now as they slept together on the floor by the bed, the fiddle case lay between them. Even in sleep it seemed Sean would not let it go, for his arm was tight around it pulling it to him.

The two ladies stood by the open door, the light from their lamps casting a yellow glow over the children. 'Poor sweet children,' said Miss Martha.

'They need a refuge, Henry. They need us.'

'Then we shall keep them as long as they need us,' said Miss Henry. 'And what do you think is so precious about that violin, Martha? That young man clutches it as if it were a part of him.'

'Perhaps it is because it has been their life blood,' said Miss Martha. 'Without it they'd have perished in the streets and cellars of Boston long ago like so many others.'

'I have to say, it was a fine idea of yours, Martha dear,' said Miss Henry. 'A fine idea, and I think I'm beginning to be glad that you deceived me into it.'

'I knew you would be,' said Martha, smiling over her lamp at her sister. 'As Little Luke says, you've a heart of gold under all that bluster.'

'Stuff and nonsense, stuff and nonsense. Now I have them here, I tell you, Martha, I shall educate them. I shall teach them how to hold a knife and fork, how to sleep in a bed. Can you imagine what kind of life they must have had, Martha, if they've never before slept in a bed? Can you imagine that? We shall give them a Christmas they will never forget, shall we not, Martha dear?'

'We shall,' said Martha. 'We shall.'

* * *

Christmas at 'The Red House', for that is how it was known everywhere in Boston, was indeed one to remember. At early Mass, the congregation buzzed with excitement as Miss Henry and Miss Martha swept down the aisle with Sean and Annie between them. Miss Henry explained them away after Mass as her 'Christmas presents', and that only fuelled the speculation.

With coloured popcorn festooned amongst the hanging greenery, the house rang with laughter and music from dawn to dusk. Blind-man's-buff and hide-and-seek began after breakfast, at which Miss Henry successfully instructed both children in the proper use of a fork. Lunch was a great feast of turkey and ham and sausagemeat, with sweet potatoes; but there was so much of it that Annie could not do it justice, with or without a fork. Sean, however, was learning to eat more slowly and cleared his plate more than once. In the afternoon cousins and aunts and uncles arrived, all bearing gifts, and they stayed to dance away the evening in the great hall with the log fires roaring up the chimneys.

But just before midnight came the great moment of the evening when, to warm applause, Little Luke and Bessie ushered the two children downstairs to the floor of the great hall. And there, Sean took the fiddle out from under his arm and set Annie dancing. She wore no longer the rough clothes of the street, but instead, Martha's white moon-shawl and a dress of maroon silk that she lifted as she danced to reveal, not satin slippers but the great black boots that she would under no circumstances be parted from. And around her neck she wore the golden torc that glowed in the orange light of the fire. For many minutes the assembled company watched enchanted and mesmerised by the precision of her footwork and the ecstasy on her face. But they could not stand still for long, and soon there was no one in the hall who was not dancing with her, except for Little Luke and Bessie who stood clapping on the staircase looking down at the mass of colour swirling below them.

'Bessie,' said Little Luke, 'there's somethin' about those children, they brings happiness wherever they go. Why you jus' look at Miss Henry, have you ever seen her dancin' before? An' she's laughin', Bessie. I seen her smile once or twice, but laughin', never laughin'. Don't she always sit by the fire at Christmas glowerin' and wishin' everyone'd go home? You 'member, Bessie? And jus' look at her now.' Miss Henry was dancing alongside Annie, her skirts held above her ankles, her feet tapping and pointing with Annie's.

'Faster, young man, faster,' she called, but Sean was already playing as fast as he could go.

'An' Bessie,' said Little Luke, 'where they get that golden necklace lil' Miss Annie's wearin'?'

'Maybe Miss Henry give it, or maybe Miss Martha,' said Bessie, 'though I ain't seen it before. She was already wearin' it when I dressed her up.'

Both Miss Henry and Miss Martha had noticed the necklace, but said nothing until they came into their room to say goodnight to them. All the guests had gone and the house was quiet once more. The children lay on the floor under a mass of blankets, with the fiddle case resting between them.

'Miss Henry,' said Annie, sitting up suddenly. 'Miss Henry, Miss Martha, that was the very best day of my life, 'ceptin maybe the day we built the house back in Ireland and Father finished the chimney. I 'member that Mother gave me the gold torc to wear that night, just for a while. But she's dead now and so 'tis mine.'

'The golden torc?' said Miss Henry. 'You mean the necklace you were wearing this evening?'

'Father says it might be more'n a thousand years

old,' said Sean. ' 'Twas worn by the first O'Brien chieftain's wife, when we owned great lands and forests all of our own. So long as we keep the torc, then the O'Briens will never die out, not in a thousand more years. Father told me once it had the power to preserve the life of those to whom it rightly belongs, and to destroy anyone who steals it.' He took out his fiddle, shook it until the gold appeared and he could hook it out carefully with his finger. 'We keep it hidden – 'tis the only safe place. Fiddler Donnelly thought of it, but then you wouldn't know about Fiddler, would you? I shall tell you one day. I told Annie she wasn't to wear it, to keep it hidden, but she's righter than me about people and she said that as you had taken us in off the street, we should have no secrets from you.' And he held out the torc in both hands.

For some reason neither Miss Henry nor Miss Martha dared to touch it, much as they wanted to, for it shone like a halo in the light of their lamp, and both felt that there was something almost holy about it. 'To be trusted with such a secret is indeed an honour, young man. We shall tell no one, you can be sure of that.'

'You can tell Little Luke and Bessie,' said Annie,

'for they must be two of the goodest people that ever lived.'

'The best,' said Miss Henry. 'Two of the best, Annie. Indeed they are, indeed they are. Now go to sleep, both of you.'

When the door had closed, the two children lay silent in the dark. 'I wonder where we shall be next Christmas,' said Annie.

'We shall be with Father in California,' said Sean.

'But just 'spose he's not there or we can't find him,' Annie said, propping herself up on her elbows. 'No one's ever heard of him in Boston. What happens when we get to 'Fornia and he's not there, or he's somewhere else, or even nowhere? He might be dead like Mother. He could have caught the plague, he could, Sean, he could.'

'Not Father,' said Sean. 'I've been thinking about it. I think that was why he left Boston so quickly, so's to avoid it. I think he's out there in California now. I think he's waiting for us to come.'

'We could stay here, Sean,' Annie said, 'we could, couldn't we? Miss Henry and Miss Martha like us well enough and I like them, and it's a lovely house and there's food and there's clothes and I'm warm in bed. I could stay here for ever.'

'No we could not, Annie,' said Sean sharply. 'We might like to, but we must not. If we did we'd never see Father again, would we now?' Annie did not answer him. She lay down on her side and covered her head with the blankets. 'All right, Annie, I shall ask Miss Henry if we can stay until spring. That'll be three months, Annie, maybe four. We can't travel much 'till then anyway. That would be something Annie, would it not?'

Annie's head came up out of the blankets. 'I shall try a bed,' she said. 'Bessie says that only critturs sleep on the floor, and I ain't no crittur,' and she climbed in between the sheets and pulled the blankets up to her nose. ''Tis almost like floating up here,' she said. 'Sean, sure 'tis almost like floating on water. Sean? Sean?' But Sean was so fast asleep that he did not even wake when the pillow she threw at him fell on his legs.

CHAPTER 17

THOSE PERFECT WEEKS AT 'THE RED HOUSE' stretched into months and spring began to encroach doggedly on winter, early crocuses piercing the frosty ground. The children spent much of their time with Little Luke and Bessie so that Annie was to become a competent cook and seamstress, often against her will. But she loved so much being with Bessie that any task was worth the doing. Annie liked well enough the baking of cakes and the mixing of pastry, but she was rather more reluctant to wash the dishes and baulked obstinately when it came to washing the kitchen floor. But Bessie kept her to it, at one point chasing her round the kitchen with the rolling pin.

Annie was too fast for her and Bessie discovered that the bribe of a slice of apple tart did more than all the threats. They would chatter on for hours in the sewing room and here it was that Annie first heard about the slaves in the cotton plantations in the South where Bessie had come from, and about the Indians that hunted the buffalo on the great plains, and the wagon trains that were rolling further west each year to open up the country that was so wide from ocean to ocean that it took a year or more to cross.

Little Luke took Sean with him wherever he went so that by spring he knew and understood horses so well that no further teaching was needed. Sean watched him move around the horses talking to them all the while with such gentleness that he had merely to imitate in order to succeed. He fed them, groomed them, rode them and drove them. He cleaned the harness and mucked out the stables once a day. Little Luke was tireless in his care and attention, as gentle to Sean as he was with the horses. He would not speak of himself nor of his past, but talked endlessly and glowingly of Miss Henry and Miss Martha, about the great furniture store in town that their father had begun and of the men they nearly married but did not because they would not leave each other or the store. And it was Little Luke who first told Sean of the black sheep of the family who never came home and whom no one ever mentioned, their little brother, Colonel Paul, a soldier of fortune who had fought the British, the Mexicans and the Indians. He was the Captain, it seemed, of what Miss Henry called 'a ship of iniquity', a river boat on the Ohio River. Little Luke was a good listener too and Sean told him of the terrible times in Ireland and about Danny and Mary and little Joe. Somehow he found he could talk more openly to Little Luke even than to Annie, for this was a man he felt who understood instinctively and who radiated sympathy but never pity.

Miss Henry and Miss Martha went every day down into Boston to the store and spent much time in an unremitting search for the children's father. Fortunately they had friends in high places, in most of the Government departments. Enquiries were extensive, but no trace whatever could be found of the Irishman, Patrick O'Brien. They knew as they searched that to discover that Patrick O'Brien had indeed passed through Boston would mean the early departure of their beloved children, but they never gave up for they also knew how anxious the children were for news of their father. They saw the wretched disappointment on their faces when each investigation proved as fruitless as the last.

When one day in early April they decided that all hope of discovering his whereabouts was finally exhausted, Miss Henry and Miss Martha knew they had to come to a decision. They went for a long walk together in the woods below the house. The children watched them from their window. They had sensed a growing solemnity about the house for several days now. They had noticed that neither Miss Henry nor Miss Martha had talked easily with them. Dinner was eaten that evening in an awkward silence that even Annie feared to break. Little food was eaten and for the first time the children heard Miss Henry snap at Bessie when she forgot to bring the white sauce for the fish.

At last she pushed away her plate and stood up. 'Children,' she said and took a deep breath. 'For three months now we have looked high and low for any trace of your father. We have circulated his description widely in Boston. It is remotely possible he passed through here a year ago, but we feel it is most unlikely. Someone surely would have remembered such a striking-looking man. What is quite certain is that he is not here now. He could have gone on to California – we do not know. If you set off to look for him you would very probably die before you reached California – many people do. Such a journey would be foolish and I could not allow you to embark upon it. And even if you got there and you found his valley, he himself may well not be there. Many things can happen to a man between Boston and California. My sister Martha and I have talked of little else for the past weeks, and this afternoon we decided we would ask you to stay and make your home with us at "The Red House". You would grow up in this house. We should send you to the best schools in Boston and we would care for you as if you were our own.' Sean was about to speak. 'Say nothing now, dear boy. Go to bed, talk about it together and you will tell us your decision when we meet again at breakfast.'

They did indeed talk until the small hours of the morning. It took that long for Sean to persuade Annie that what they were about to do was the only thing they could do. Sean wanted to tell them their decision at breakfast but Annie would not hear of it. 'If we're going,' she said, 'we'll go now whilst they're asleep. I'll not look them in the face and tell them we're going. I could not do it, Sean. Sure I could not bear the hurt in their eyes.'

It was Sean's idea to sit down and compose the letter explaining why they had to go, why they could not stay. They both signed it and left it on the table in the great hall as they stole out of the house before dawn, the fiddle case under Sean's arm.

They had almost reached the front gate when a shadow moved out of the darkness and stood before them. 'Miss Martha said you'd be goin'.' It was Little Luke's deep voice and they could just make out the silhouette of his derby hat against the night sky. 'She told me I wasn't to let you go without breakfast. She's waitin' for you in the kitchen children; an' you never said goodbye to my Bessie – she's goin' to be mighty upset, children, mighty upset; an' when she's upset I gets it in the ear an' that ain't funny. No sir, that ain't funny at all.'

CHAPTER 18

MISS HENRY AND MISS MARTHA WERE SITTING side by side at the kitchen table, the only oil lamp in the room lighting their faces. On the table in front of them lay the letter that Sean had written less than an hour before. Bessie fussed around them as they came in, cuddling each of them in turn. 'What you go an' do a thing like that for?' she said. 'Where d'you think you was agoin' to, out there in the middle of the night?'

'Come and stand where I can see you,' said Miss Henry. She sounded sad and tired. 'And do stop fussing them, Bessie. Closer, closer; so I can see your faces. That's better. So,' she went on, 'Martha was right again. She said you'd try to run off. She said you'd go. She knew you wouldn't stay with us. I'm a foolish old woman – no, no; everyone thinks so – and now I know so. You see children, I thought I could tempt you into abandoning your father. I was wrong, and I don't care to be wrong. It vexes me. So you'll go whatever I say to persuade you to the contrary, is that right?'

'Yes, Miss Henry,' said Sean quietly. 'We have to.'

'Children,' Miss Henry said, leaning forward across the table. 'It is perhaps three thousand miles across a wild continent peopled with wild and wicked men and marauding savages, and at the end of it the probability that you will never find your father, alive or dead. And you still will go?'

'Yes, Miss Henry,' said Sean.

'Very well, then we must adopt Martha's plan. Mine was to keep you here, but I can see that has failed. You will need a wagon and provisions. We would take you ourselves, would we not, Martha, but we find the trip into Boston quite exhausting, and that's just four miles. We are both too old and too feeble for such a journey.'

'Miss Henry,' Little Luke interrupted. 'What is you thinkin' of, sendin' out these two children without anyone to look after 'em? You cain't do it, Miss Henry. It ain't right.'

'You're quite right,' said Miss Henry. 'Quite right, Little Luke, and that is why we were going to ask you to take our place. I want you to take these two children of ours down to Wheeling, Ohio and hand them over into the safe-keeping of my despicable brother. I shall write to him and appeal to his better nature. It is the only thing I have ever asked of him. It is a journey of a thousand miles, perhaps more, and is therefore not to be undertaken lightly. You are a free man, Little Luke, have been since the day you came here with Bessie thirty years ago. As a free man you do not have to do what I am asking you. You understand, Little Luke?'

'Yes, Miss Henry,' said Little Luke, somewhat doubtfully. 'I'm thinkin' 'bout that.'

'Well, Little Luke, you're unusually silent. What have you to say?'

'Well, Miss Henry, when I upped and ran away with my Bessie from Virginia all that while ago, it was only 'cos she tol' me it was the best thing to do. Ever since then I found it 'spedient to ask my Bessie and do 'zactly what she says. She ain't never bin wrong yet, not in my reckonin'.'

'How long you be gone, Luke?' Bessie asked.

'A few months,' said Little Luke. 'Back by the Fall, should be.'

'So you're goin'?' said Bessie.

'You knows I is, woman,' Little Luke took her hand gently. 'You knows I is. But I'd feel a whole lot better if you tell me I's right to go.'

'You is right. You know you is right,' Bessie said. 'It's the best way an' the only way to help these children find their papa. So why you ask?'

' 'Cos I likes to hear you agreein' with me, Bessie.'

'Well, I'm agreein' ain't I? But don't 'spect me to be pleased about it, 'cos I ain't. I ain't never bin without him for thirty years, Miss Annie, so you be sure'n look after him for me and send him back all in one piece before them leaves begin to fall.' And Bessie turned away to hide her face.

'Don't be sad, Bessie,' said Annie, putting her arm around her. 'We'll not let anything happen to him, will we Sean?'

'I ain't sad 'bout him, Annie child, I knows he'll come home. Ain't nothin' gonna stop my Luke from comin' back to me. I'm sad on account of you're our children and you're goin', an' you ain't never comin' back. But you gonna find your papa, I knows it. An' when you do, you tells him that if he don't want to keep you, he gotta send you right back here any time, ain't that right, Miss Henry?'

'It most surely is, Bessie,' said Miss Henry. 'Whether you come back to us or not, this will always be your home.' And she stood up and clapped her hands. 'Very well, so there's work to be done. You must leave at sun-up. You'll take the chuck wagon, Little Luke, and two good horses, Bella and Beau I suggest. They're the strongest. You'll need provisions for a month and all the blankets and clothes you can carry. Martha will see to that, won't you Martha? And Bessie, I want you to see to the provisions. They are to have everything they need. It will be a long journey, a very long journey.'

The clear night had left a covering of frost that caught the sun and turned the world pink at dawn. At the last moment Miss Martha put her best white moon-shawl around Annie's head and kissed her fondly on both cheeks. Neither could bring themselves to say anything. Miss Henry presented Sean with a gleaming black revolver that lay cold and heavy in his hands. 'Just in case you ever need it,' she whispered. 'It was my father's and he would want you to have it. Bring it back one day if you are passing by.' And she pushed the hair out of his eyes before standing back away from the wagon. Little Luke sat stiffly beside them and never turned to wave as they did.

'We won't see them again, Sean, will we?' said Annie as the wagon rumbled away down the drive. But Sean would not answer her.

CHAPTER 19

LITTLE LUKE DID NOT SPEAK ALL THAT FIRST morning but sat staring ahead of him. Beside him Sean sat with the fiddle case across his lap. He was consumed with doubts about the decision he had made. Only Annie talked of how she would come back when she was older and knock on their door and surprise them all. 'Little Luke,' she went on, 'will it be far to go?'

'Far enough, lil' missy, far enough. All the way down through Pennsylvania to Wheelin', Ohio. That's as far as I'm takin' you. I got a letter to Colonel Paul from Miss Henry. He's gonna take you on his river-boat all the way to St. Louis and up the

Missouri River, and then you gotta go some more, I dunno how far 'cos I ain't bin there. An' if you goes on talkin' like that all the way, you'll talk yo'self dumb before you git there.'

'Why did Miss Henry give me her father's gun?' Sean asked, bringing it out from under his coat. 'Sure I've never ever fired a gun.'

'Well I'm gonna teach you, Master Sean, 'cos you're gonna need it. Somewhere 'tween here and that California of yours, you're gonna need it, so I'm gonna teach you.'

'And me? Will I be learning to shoot too?' Annie asked.

'Ain't proper, lil' missy. Guns ain't proper things for no young lady, no sir, not proper at all.' Annie protested vehemently, but Little Luke was adamant.

'Now I's just gone an' left my Bessie, lil' missy, an' I'm feelin' sad as hell; so why don' you git out your fiddle Master Sean and you Miss Annie, you kin sing me somethin' to cheer up my spirits. 'Sgonna be a long, hard road, chil, a long hard road. We's gonna git there sure's my name's Lil' Luke. I'm gonna find that Colonel Paul down at Wheelin', Ohio, an' I'm gonna ride back up this very same road 'fore the winter comes in, 'cos if I don't, my

Bessie will eat me 'live.' And Little Luke's great beaming smile shone out once again and they laughed with him.

It was that smile that saw them through every difficulty they encountered on their journey. There were endless days of mud and rain, when the wagon wheels sank to the axle. There were the long dark nights by the camp fire, and the sounds of the forest threatening around them. He was engineer, navigator, doctor, veterinary surgeon, hunter, cook and father and all with endless optimism and cheerfulness.

He taught them to build a fire, to skin cottontails and squirrels, to pick pigeons and turkeys, to make coffee thick and strong like soup. He was as good as his word and taught Sean how to clean his revolver, how to load it, cock it and fire it. And of course Annie managed to take her turn, although the revolver was too heavy for her to hold it still. 'Sure frightens the hell out of me,' Little Luke said, closing his eyes as she pulled the trigger. 'And I'm behind the gun!'

In return for all this he would ask only one thing. In the evenings he would sit with his back against a treetrunk and Sean would take out his fiddle and play for him, and Annie would put on the golden torc, throw her moonshawl over her shoulders and dance for him. Afterwards Little Luke would wrap it carefully in a cloth and push it gently back into the fiddle. 'Won't rattle so much that way,' he would say.

The Pennsylvania country they passed through that spring seemed so rich and bountiful to the children, with its great forests alive with game, its rivers teeming with silver fish. Tidy, fertile farmsteads stretched along the sheltered valleys, hewn out of the forests that themselves climbed up into cloud-covered mountains. It was hard to understand why anyone should pass through such a place and more than once they asked after their father, just in case he had had the same idea and had stopped to farm in this paradise.

As they moved further south into the summer the roads hardened and in spite of bruising ruts and pot-holes they moved on with increasing speed – over thirty miles they covered some days before making camp for the night.

Little Luke would leave them only to go hunting. Sean had begged him time and again to take him, but Little Luke was not to be persuaded. 'One person's got jus' two feet, two person's got four; and two persons always smell twice as bad to a crittur,' he'd say. 'Besides, you got them horses to see to and they're hungry and thirsty; and besides that there's lil' Miss Annie – you ain't gonna leave her all by herself are you? You gotta stay an' look after her like a good brother should. She's only little so you cain't 'spect her to do all the cookin' by herself. My Bessie's taught her an' she's a good cook, but she ain't that good. Now don' you dare go tellin' her I said so.' So Sean stood each evening as dusk fell and watched enviously as Little Luke vanished into the trees with his rifle.

On just such an evening they were camped by a stream in a deserted valley only a few miles east of Pittsburgh. The flies which had been bothering them more and more as they moved south, hummed around their heads as Sean and Annie led the horses down to the stream to drink. 'I'll bring them back, Annie,' said Sean. 'Will you be getting the fire going? They'll eat us alive tonight if we don't smoke them out. If there's one thing I could do without in this country, Annie, 'tis the flies. I tell you, Annie, there's not a bit of me they haven't eaten. I think they're partial to Irish blood. Must be that 'cos they never go near Little Luke.' But Annie was looking past him into the trees. 'Is something the matter, Annie?'

'The trees, they moved. I tell you they moved. There's someone in the trees, I know there is. Listen.'

'Sure 'tis just the wind, Annie,' said Sean, paying her scant attention. 'The wind gets up most evenings, I've noticed that.'

'But I did hear someone,' Annie insisted angrily. 'And I know they were looking at us.' Sean scanned the trees more to placate his sister than anything else, and saw nothing.

'Maybe, 'tis someone camped further up the valley,' he said. 'The road's been full of people these last weeks. More every day. All going west, Little Luke says. Sound will carry along a valley, you know. 'Tis nothing, Annie, nothing at all.'

'Sean, d'you 'member that man who rode past us yesterday? 'Member I told you he kept looking back at us and smiling, 's'if he knew us maybe. An' you said he was just being friendly, and Little Luke said he smiled only with his mouth and that he did not like people who smiled only with their mouths? Well, I think it's him. He was wearing a wide-brimmed hat and a jerkin with all them shredded bits hanging down, 'member? 'Tis him, Sean, I know 'tis.'

But Sean was far too busy controlling the two

horses to listen to her any more. It did not for one moment occur to him that his sister might be right. After all, only the day before she had sworn blind that someone was following them, and Little Luke had even stopped, unhitched Bella from the wagon and gone off to search. He had found nothing.

'Annie,' he said, 'we have to get the horses fed and watered and the fire lit before Little Luke gets back. Stop your nonsense now and come on and help.'

All that evening Annie sat silent by the fire. She would neither cook nor eat the cottontail Little Luke had brought back, and she would not dance or sing for him either. She sat cross-legged and sullen, glaring into the fire; and neither Little Luke nor Sean could persuade her there was nothing to worry about. When they curled up together under the chuck-wagon that night, she was so eaten up with fury that she would not say goodnight to either of them. She lay awake in her anger almost until dawn and then fell into a deep sleep.

She was woken suddenly by the neighing of horses and sat up in time to see Beau galloping off down the track and out of sight. Only then did she realise that Little Luke and Sean were no longer beside her. She crawled out from under the wagon calling for them, and she knew by the tone of their voices when they replied that something was wrong. Both of them were standing by the smoking embers of the fire, their hands high in the air. 'Nice an' easy, little girl,' said a hard voice behind her. 'I don't want to hurt no one, not 'less I have to.' A warm shiver of alarm ran up her spine as he spoke and she knew even before she turned to look that she would find the man who had been following them. She felt no satisfaction in being right, only a deep sense of indignation that no one had listened to her. The voice did indeed belong to the man in the shredded leather jerkin and the wide-brimmed hat who was now pointing his rifle at her head.

CHAPTER 20

'MISS ANNIE, YOU COME RIGHT OVER HERE BY me,' said Little Luke quickly. 'He won't hurt you none. He just wanna take our things, that's all. An' things ain't that important, not 'nough to git killed for anyhow. Anyways, he won't find nothin' in that ole wagon 'cos like told him, we ain't got nothin' 'cept a few blankets.'

'That's where you're wrong, nigger-man,' said the man, stepping towards them, his spurs clanking as he came. 'Sure I'm gonna have a little look through your wagon case there's somethin' worth havin' in there. But it's you I'm after, nigger-man. I trades in niggers. Bounty hunter they calls me. I comes up north every summer, catches me a fine crop of runaway slaves and I sells them fifty dollars apiece back down south. All I gotta do is git you down into Kentucky and there's folk there'll pay me more'n fifty dollars for runaways. Better trade than horse thievin' 'cos it's legal an' you don't git hung for it. They got cotton down there an' they ain't 'nough people to pick it, so I's takin' you back home, nigger-man.'

'I'm a free man,' said Little Luke. 'I bin free for thirty years or more.'

'All niggers is slaves, nigger-man, don't you know that yet? You born a slave, you die a slave. Now you kin die right here if you've a mind to, or you kin git on that horse and ride out with me nice an' easy.'

'Don't go, Little Luke,' Annie cried, running over to him and standing in front of him. 'Don't go.'

'Annie, lil' Miss Annie,' said Little Luke, crouching down to her height. 'The man's got my rifle. There ain't nothin' I kin do, and what's more, there ain't nothin' you kin do. Should've heeded you, Miss Annie. Sean and me, should've heeded you. Now you go right back home to Boston and tell my Bessie I'll be just fine, you hear me now?'

'Mister?' said Sean, speaking with calm deliberation. 'If we were to have something maybe worth fifty dollars or more, would you take that instead?'

The bounty hunter looked long at Sean before he spoke. Then he smiled. ' 'Pends on what you got, son.'

'Don't do it Master Sean,' said Little Luke. 'You cain't make no bargains with the devil. Don't do it.'

But Sean ignored him. ' 'Tis gold, mister,' said Sean. 'If I let you have it will you promise to let Little Luke go and leave us alone?'

'If it's worth more'n fifty dollars, son, then you got a deal. But I gotta see it first.'

'Shall I be fetching it then?' said Sean.

'Let the girl do it,' said the man, motioning at Annie with his rifle.

'Fetch it, Annie,' said Sean. And Annie obeyed instantly for she knew this was the only chance of saving Little Luke. She crawled in under the wagon, lifted the blanket and there, beside the fiddle case, where they always kept it, lay Sean's revolver. 'Have you got it, Annie?' she heard Sean call, and she knew what he meant.

'Got it,' she said, stuffing the revolver into her shirt. She came out carrying the fiddle case in both arms and laid it on the ground.

'So it's a fiddle, a golden fiddle is it?' said the bounty hunter. 'Stop wasting my time.'

'Open it, Annie,' said Sean. 'Take it out and show him.' Annie hooked out the torc with her little finger, unwrapped it and held it up in the air. She waited until he took the torc and held it up to his mouth to bite it. At that moment the barrel of his rifle wavered and lowered and Annie knew this was the chance she had been waiting for. She whipped the revolver out from under her shirt.

'Mister, you drop that rifle and throw down the torc, else I'll shoot you, mister, I will, I'll shoot you.' The weight of the revolver made her hands tremble, but the bounty hunter just looked down at her from under his wide-brimmed hat and laughed; and Annie knew from the confidence in the laugh that she had made a mistake.

'Little girl, ain't you forgotten somethin'? Ain't you forgotten to cock it?' And as he spoke she knew she had. He simply reached out and took the revolver from her hand.

Sean was forced to tie Little Luke's hands behind his back as he sat astride Bella. Then, with the torc in his saddle bag and Sean's revolver in his belt, the man turned to them, a sneering smile creasing his unshaven face. 'Don't you worry none, I'll take real good care of him. He's worth more to me 'live than dead, but even 'live he ain't worth the gold in that necklace of your'n. Why there's 'nough gold in that necklace to buy ten of him. So I'll take real good care of that too. Be seein' you friends, I'm obliged, mighty obliged.'

Little Luke smiled sadly. 'You done all you could, children, you tried mighty hard an' you cain't do no more. Go home now like I said, an' you tell my Bessie I'm comin' home just the same.' And they rode away leaving the children under the trees with the ransacked wagon, the fiddle, and the embers of a dying fire.

'We promised Bessie we'd look after him,' said Annie, fighting back tears of hopeless rage. 'We promised her, and now he's gone and our torc has gone with him. Everything's gone.'

'Not quite, Annie,' said Sean, pointing up into the trees. Beau stood snuffling at the grass at the edge of the wood. 'We still have him, and we still have the fiddle.'

'But he can't be pulling the wagon all by himself. 'Tis too heavy. He'd be too slow and we'd never catch them.'

'No need for the wagon, Annie, Beau could carry the two of us and the fiddle, could he not?'

'But even if we catch them up, what can we do? Sure he's got Little Luke's rifle and he's got your revolver. What can we do?' And she stamped her foot. 'Oh why did I forget to cock it?'

'T'wouldn't have helped, Annie,' said Sean walking slowly away towards Beau holding his hand out. 'Wasn't loaded anyway. Little Luke always unloads it. I thought you knew that.' Annie was not sure whether that made it better or worse, but she certainly found very little comfort in it. 'What's done is done, Annie. Every minute we stay talking here Little Luke and the torc are moving away from us further and further. We can't go back to Bessie without Little Luke, can we now, and we couldn't face Father without the torc. So pick up the fiddle, Annie, and everything we can carry, and I'll catch Beau – that's if he'll let me.'

CHAPTER 21

THAT NIGHT THE WIND BLEW THE CLOUDS ACROSS the face of the moon and sent them scudding through the heavens. It whipped through the trees in wild and angry gusts, shaking the leaves into a frenzy, so that sleep for the bounty hunter was quite impossible. Little Luke lay trussed up on the ground, his hands and feet tied so tight that he could scarcely feel them. He was haunted by the terrible prospect of slavery, by thoughts of the two children he had left alone and defenceless on the trail and by memories of his dear Bessie in her yellow apron. He cursed the wind for keeping the bounty hunter awake and concentrated on finding a stone sharp enough to chafe away at the bindings on his wrists, but the search proved fruitless and he lay back impotent and frustrated. He had all but given up any hope of escape when, in the early hours of the morning, he heard through the noise of the storm a strange, unearthly sound grating on the wind.

'D'you hear that?' whispered the bounty hunter, throwing off his blanket and getting to his feet, rifle in hand. 'D'you hear that? Did you hear it?'

'Cain't hear nothin',' Little Luke said. 'I cain't hear nothin'.' Little Luke hoped, but dared not believe in what he hoped, until the sound came again, as it did, closer now, a shrill and steely whine.

'You deaf, nigger-man? Cain't you hear it?' And the bounty hunter crouched over him.

'I did that time,' said Little Luke, trying to suppress the excitement in his voice. 'And I'm afraid, mighty afraid. Ain't you heard 'bout them Injuns, 'bout how them Injuns when they attack just 'fore dawn, they sends out their ghosts to scare the livin' daylights out of folk?'

'But there ain't any hostiles, not around these parts,' said the bounty hunter. 'Is there?'

'Then maybe they jus' gone an' left their ghosts behind 'em,' said Little Luke. 'An' I'm afraid, mighty

afraid. I don't wanna lose my scalp. There it is again.'
It was closer this time, a dreadful howl like a
wounded coyote; and then through the trees floated a
white sepulchral figure, its shrouds standing out in
the wind, arms upraised and flitting from tree to tree.
The bounty hunter fired his rifle blindly into the
woods again and again, but the eerie music played
on, more insistent now and louder.

'It's comin' for us,' cried Little Luke, his voice
trembling with terror. 'It's comin' for us, Lord
preserve us. An' they's the scalpin' kind, I knows they
is.'

The bounty hunter was backing away now
towards the horses, firing wildly as he went at the
white apparition that seemed now to be pointing at
him as it moved through the darkness and vanished
once more, and all the while the dreadful screeching
sound filled the air around him. He did not stay even
to saddle the horse, but leapt up and dug his heels
into the horse's side and was gone into the darkness.

No sooner was he gone than the dreadful music
ceased. 'You ain't afoolin' me, children,' Little Luke
called out. 'I's heard you go wrong on that fiddle
often 'nough to know what it sounds like. An' Miss
Annie I knowed it's you playin' it cos I heard you try

once before – 'nough to scare the bugs out of a cat.'

'Are you sure he's gone, Little Luke?' It was Sean's voice from under the white moon-shawl.

'Master Sean, you gone an' scared him so's he won't ever come back. Now if it ain't too much trouble, I'd be mighty obliged if you'd git down here an' untie me.'

Annie rubbed his feet for him until he began to feel them again. 'Did he treat you bad, Little Luke?'

'Didn't feed me a whole lot,' said Little Luke, rubbing his wrists and stretching his cramped fingers. 'But I don't bruise easy. There's always been folk like him, always will be. Where there's water there's leeches. But you gotta go careful, children, real careful, 'cos he ain't the only one like that.'

'I was,' said Annie, hands on hips and triumphant at last. 'I was carefuller than the both of you.'

'So you was,' said Little Luke. 'That sister of yours, she ain't no little girl no more, Master Sean.'

'S'pose not,' Sean said, putting his arm around her. 'But the fiddle playing in the trees, that was my idea.'

'Sure the white ghost was mine,' Annie retorted. 'And 'twas my moon-shawl.'

Throughout the planning and execution of the

rescue attempt neither Annie nor Sean had given a thought to the torc. They had perhaps assumed that the rescue of one meant recovery of the other. And even now, they were so happy and amazed at their own success, and so relieved to be with Little Luke again, that all other considerations were as nothing.

At last Little Luke stood up and stamped around for a few moments until the feeling returned to his feet again. Then he bent down and kissed each one of them in turn. 'That's from my Bessie,' he said. 'An' that's from me. An' I ain't a kissin' kind of man, 'member that now. We got nothin' else to give you children, wish we had. I ain't gonna show it, I may even keep smilin', but when I says goodbye to you two, I'm gonna be mighty sad, mighty sad. But well as that, Lil' Luke's gonna be a happy man 'cos he knows he got two of the best friends a man ever had, an' what's more, he knows after what you just done you don't need no Lil' Luke, you don't need no one to look after you no more. You gonna be fine on your own, just fine, children. Why, you kin drive the horses, cook the beans, play the fiddle, sing and dance like a princess and see off bounty hunters without ever firin' a shot. Ain't nothin' gonna stop you children, nothin'. Why, that bounty hunter, he left so fast he ain't even got his boots on.' And he held up a pair of ragged boots with turned-up toes. 'Took his rifle, his horse and his saddle bags – 's'all he had time for with them ghostly Injuns chasin' him . . .'

'Did you say he had the saddle bags with him, Little Luke?' said Sean, putting a hand on his arm.

'Just that, no time for nothin' else. Blankets still here, saddle still here,' said Little Luke. And then suddenly he too realised the implications of what he had said.

''Tis where he kept the torc, is it not?' Annie said, knowing it full well. 'He still has it then.'

As dawn filtered down through the trees they searched the ground minutely just in case it had fallen out, but they found nothing. The revolver Miss Henry had given Sean was gone too.

'He took all Miss Henry's money too, 's'all in that saddle bag,' said Little Luke. 'We ain't got nothin' left, children.'

'We got you,' said Annie.

But their triumph had turned suddenly sour. In disappointed silence they rode back all that day to the place where they had left the wagon, and the following morning they were on their way South once again. Hungry, tired and dispirited they travelled on down through Pittsburgh until they struck the road that took them into Wheeling itself a few days later.

Little Luke and the children rode into the straggling town in the cool of the evening, the fiddle case clutched firmly at Sean's knee. Half the world it seemed was heading for Wheeling, some of them in wagons, some on horseback and some on foot, driving their farm stock ahead of them; and there were dogs, dogs everywhere.

'Well, children, that's what we come for, the great Ohio River,' said Little Luke, as they turned into the main street. 'Seems like you ain't the only ones goin' west.'

'He'll be here somewhere,' said Sean, looking around him for a wide-brimmed hat and a shredded leather jerkin. 'That bounty hunter, he'll be here. He's got to be here.'

'Ain't no way you gonna find that man, Master Sean,' said Little Luke. 'So you'd best stop lookin'. An' what you gonna do if you find him, or if he finds you? We ain't got no gun 'tween us. We's 'live, ain't we; I'm 'live an' a free man thanks to you, an' soon's I find that Colonel Paul you gonna be safe as houses. Miss Henry said I'd be bound to find the Colonel in the saloon on the main street – spends most of his time a drinkin' an' a gamblin' she said. This here's the main street, but it seems like there's a whole lot of saloons round here, an' they's full to burstin'.' And sure enough there were a dozen or more saloons to be found in the town in amongst the gunsmiths, the saddlers, the grocery stores and hotels.

With Sean and Annie always close behind him he searched every saloon for Colonel Paul. Everyone knew him well enough and smiled at the mention of his name, but no one it seemed knew where he could be found.

They soon lost count of the number of saloons they had searched, and Annie was stumbling with fatigue and hunger when Little Luke and Sean climbed the steps into the last saloon on the street. She sat down on the steps outside to wait for them, her head on her arms.

Some minutes later the swing doors of the saloon were thrown open and as Annie looked up over her shoulder at the wedge of bright light, a tall, elegant man in a grey suit emerged, one hand hooked in his waistcoat pocket, the other holding a long cigar that glowed as he drew on it and lit up his face. It was a stern, frowning face that looked down at Annie.

'And you, I suppose, would be Annie O'Brien,' said the man in grey, rearranging the chain of his gold fob watch. His tone, like his face, was distant and disinterested.

'I am,' said Annie, getting to her feet.

'Sister Henry and Sister Martha wrote me a letter, Miss O'Brien, a letter that Little Luke has just given to me. I am their brother, Colonel Paul Whitman, and I'm told I have to take you under my wing. I can't imagine why, but no doubt my sisters have their reasons for such an absurd request. To be honest with you, Miss O'Brien, I don't much care for children – never had much to do with them. However, you will accompany me to my riverboat and I will install you and your brother in my cabin until I have decided what can be done about you. You may follow me.'

For once in her life Annie was speechless. Even when Sean and Little Luke joined her on the steps of the saloon, all she could do was open her mouth like a goldfish and point at the tall figure limping away from them down the street leaning on his cane, his cigar glowing orange in the night.

CHAPTER 22

THE COLONEL LISTENED ATTENTIVELY, BROWS furrowed, as they told their story the next morning. He sat in a red velvet-covered armchair in the spacious cabin they shared with him. Across his knees was the silver-topped cane that never left his side. Sean detected a gentleness in his hands and eyes that belied the severity of his behaviour the night before. He had the jutting chin of his sisters and the craggy, weathered look of a man of some years – not old exactly, but not young either. His hair still held the black of youth but was greying to white at the temples. He wore a trim silver moustache that he smoothed as he listened to them.

There was a long silence when they had finished. His words when they came were clipped and decisive. 'Very well,' he said, slapping the arms of his chair and pushing himself to his feet and resting on his cane. 'I have considered what can be done, and you will not like any of it. First, Little Luke must be sent back home as soon as he has rested, if he is to be back in Boston by the Fall. I shall supply you with all you need, Little Luke. You will take with you a letter to my sisters in which I will promise to see these two safely on to a wagon train heading west from Independence. That is what they asked me to do and that is what I shall do. Second, I can offer little hope that you will recover your golden torc, as you call it. There are many such scoundrels as this bounty hunter and many of them wear wide-brimmed hats – this town is full of them, wicked men who feed like vultures on the unwary and the innocent. We would be lucky indeed to find him again. As for your father, I can be no more optimistic. I have seen many thousands of red-haired Irishmen of great stature and strength, just as you describe him, many of whom are called Patrick and some of whom will even be called O'Brien, so many that it is hardly possible I, or indeed anyone, would remember him. And lastly your journey to California will take you longer than you imagine. You will have to be patient. It is already high summer, and if we leave within the week we shall be in St. Louis by the end of July, and we could be at Independence three weeks later – far too late to start out on the two thousand mile journey across the great plains towards Oregon and California. The winter would catch you and kill you, as it does so many. The spring is the time to leave, early spring. So you will have to stay with me through the winter and set off the following spring. I cannot pretend I like the arrangement, but what has to be done has to be done.'

'I'm tellin' you, children,' Little Luke said, 'you's gonna live on a real live steaming river-boat an' the Colonel here's gonna take good care of you. Ain't you, Colonel?' But Sean and Annie were not to be consoled. They were about to lose Little Luke for ever, the torc was lost to them and the hope that they might be reunited with their father that year had been extinguished utterly.

No amount of good food and rest in their opulent cabin could revive their drained spirits. The last evening before Little Luke left them, he asked them to play and dance for him once more on the deck of the river-boat, and for a few hours they lost themselves in the joy of it before the reality of the parting they dreaded came upon them. At first light, with the new wagon loaded and Beau and Bella fed and watered, Sean helped Little Luke to hitch them up, his fingers fumbling with the leathers as the tears he tried to hold back blinded him. At the last, Annie was unwilling even to release Little Luke's hand.

'You'll look after 'em, Colonel,' said Little Luke, shaking the Colonel's hand. 'I'd take you all the way, children,' he said, putting his arms around them, 'you knows I would, but my Bessie made the rules an' I gotta keep 'em – my place is beside her. You understand that? Now you keeps warm on the cold nights an' think of us all sometimes up at the Red House. An' you keep smilin'. I wants to 'member you smilin'. You ain't smilin', Miss Annie. Smile children, else I'm gonna cry too, an' that ain't good for a man.' And so he left them laughing through their tears, looked back once as he whipped up the horses and was gone.

It was therefore in Colonel Paul Whitman's river-boat, the *Henry Martha*, that Sean and Annie left for St. Louis some days later. She was a three-tiered river-boat with a mast fore and aft and a great black funnel braced between the two paddle-wheel arches that rose so high that they dwarfed even the upper decks. Perched on the top deck was the tower of the wheelhouse and the gambling saloon.

They saw little of the Colonel in the few days before departure, only at breakfast, which was a silent affair held always in his cabin. He seemed preoccupied with the preparation of the boat and had little time for them. They felt suddenly alone and deserted and longed for the warmth of Little Luke's company. But the Colonel saw to it that they were kept busy, helping to load the ship. The hold had to be filled with food and provisions for St. Louis and beyond, and they became part of the human chain that transported the boxes and crates from the dockside to the hold. The lower deck was crammed with wagons and carts, untidy piles of saddles and harnesses, and at one end there was a fenced-off area like a farmyard where the horses, mules, pigs and cows were tethered, lying down together in apparent harmony. Even the upper deck itself was covered with barrels, lashed to the handrails for safety. All the while as the boat was loaded, she lay lower and lower in the water.

In amongst all this were the passengers, on the lower decks – a crowd of shy German migrants on their way to Oregon. Then there were a few mountain men, their great bushy faces barely visible under their furs, and always, it seemed, with a clay pipe in their mouths and a rifle beside them. And on the upper deck strolled the gamblers and traders who emerged from the gambling saloon only to take the fresh air when the cigar smoke became too thick.

The children were in the wheelhouse next to their cabin when the order for steam was given, and the boat shuddered and shook as the engines got up steam and the great paddle wheels amidships began to churn. They heard the Colonel give the order to cast off and stood mesmerized as the steamer moved out into the middle of the stream, a tower of black smoke and sparks filling the air above them. They watched him as he passed among his passengers, slightly hunched and limping on his cane, a figure of great command and presence, and for whom everyone clearly felt an instinctive respect.

Neither of the children could understand how this man could be the black sheep of any family, and

Annie resolved to pluck up the courage to ask him at the earliest opportunity. This occurred at supper their first night out from Wheeling.

'Mister Colonel,' she said, as soon as they had sat down. 'Back in Boston your sister, Miss Henry, said you were 'spicable, whatever that might mean, and everyone always went quiet whenever they mentioned your name. Why did they call you 'spicable?' Sean had ceased to reprimand his sister now for her boldness – he felt she was already too old and that any influence he might have had over her behaviour was minimal. His position as the wise older brother had been much eroded over the matter of Little Luke's capture, and the loss of the torc. So he said nothing but chewed long on his meat to avoid showing his embarrassment.

'Annie O'Brien,' said the Colonel, sitting back and wiping his lips with his napkin. 'If I was to ask you to tell me the wickedest thing you had ever done, would you tell me?'

'Yes,' said Annie at once.

'Well then, you tell me first and then I shall tell you,' said the Colonel, somewhat surprised at her response to his challenge.

' 'Twas when my little brother Danny was dying

back home in Ireland,' said Annie quietly. 'I 'member I wished him dead so as I could have his food. I had lots of thoughts like that, still do. But my thoughts are wickeder than what I do.'

'That's not uncommon, Annie; 'twould be a terrible world if it were the other way around,' said the Colonel, lighting up a great cigar. Annie watched the smoke rings dissipate as they rose towards the ceiling. 'Very well, I shall tell you my secret because you have told me yours and because, as sister Henry said in her letter, I should treat you as one of the family – and it is a family secret. A story straight from the Bible, children. Maybe if I'd read it more diligently as a child I should never have gone astray. It was when I reached the age of twenty – and all this is over thirty years ago now, I well remember Little Luke and Bessie had just joined us at the Red House – I asked my father to give me my fortune, which I knew was considerable. I did not want to spend my life running a great furniture store in Boston, you see. I wanted to travel and to see the world. I wanted to make my mark on this new nation of ours. So my father, being a good and kind man, he trusted me and gave me every dollar he could spare and let me go out into the world. You should never give a young horse his head, children. Oh, I was young and rich and very foolish – a catastrophic combination. I began to gamble – and I was good, very good – or I thought I was. Within two years I had gambled away all my money and had run into debt. My father saved me from prison and sent me into the army where I made a tolerably good soldier, but he died not long after of a broken heart. My sisters, although kind enough to me at the funeral, never really forgave me for what I had done, and I have never forgiven myself. I vowed at his graveside I should never gamble again, and I have kept to that to this day. So children, that is why I am held to be the black sheep by my sisters – 'spicable, as you say, Annie.'

'Have you not been back since to Boston?' Annie asked.

The Colonel nodded. 'From time to time I have been back and stood outside the Red House, the house I was born in, and though I have longed to go inside, I have never dared. I have faced and outfaced the British soldiers, Mexicans and Indians; but my sister Henry has eyes that reach to my very soul, and I could never bring myself to look her in the eyes. So I have always walked away. Martha writes each year and asks me to go. Maybe one day I will. Do you know that this is the first time my sister Henry has written to me in a long, long time – you must be very important to her. Now enough of your questions, Annie O'Brien, there's work to be done.'

Sean, less gregarious than his sister, preferred to spend the days alone with the Colonel in the wheel-house, and it was not long before the Ohio River obliged with a stretch of clear, straight water, no snags, no sandbars – and the Colonel allowed him to take the wheel for the first time. At first it was only for a few moments, but as the days went by his confidence in the young boy multiplied. As the Colonel had made quite clear, he had never before liked children a great deal. They were, in his view, usually dirty and always, he said 'disagreeable, incompetent and only improved with age'. Sean's growing competence at the helm was already changing his mind and Annie was proving an asset to the river-boat, bringing joy and laughter wherever she went. She acted as go-between for him with the shy German migrants who would talk more easily and freely to her in their broken English, and she saw to the comfort of their animals, many of whom were in poor condition for any journey. Without anyone asking, she saw to it they always had fresh water and bedding. The colonel was surprised therefore, and not a little disappointed, when she came screaming into the wheelhouse one evening.

'Sean, Sean. I seen him. I seen him. 'Tis him for sure.'

'What Annie, who?'

''Tis the man in the wide-brimmed hat, the bounty hunter who stole our torc. I seen him. He went into the saloon. He is cleaned up some, and dressed differently, but I know 'tis him, I know it. Oh Sean, don't be doubting me. You doubted me once before. 'Tis him I tell you. Come and see, quickly.'

CHAPTER 23

'HOLD FAST, YOUNG GIRL,' SAID THE COLONEL sternly. 'No one comes bursting into my wheelhouse screaming like a wild animal. Calm yourself. Now, am I right in understanding that you believe you have seen the rogue who took Little Luke and your torc, and that he is in my gambling saloon at this moment?'

'He is, Mister Colonel, he is. As the Blessed Mary is my witness, he is. I would know that face anywhere. Oh please, Mister Colonel, you can get it back for us, can't you, Mister Colonel?' Annie went on. 'Without it we shall never reach California, and we shall never find Father, I know we won't.'

'It means a lot to you, Annie, does it not?' said the Colonel, pulling on his gloves.

'Mother once said it was the soul of our family,' Sean interposed quietly.

'Very well,' the Colonel said. 'But first we must be sure that it is indeed him. Come along.' From the windy deck outside they looked into the brightly-lit saloon.

'The one in the green jacket,' Annie whispered, stabbing at the window with her forefinger. 'Wait 'til he turns his head, you'll see, Sean.' They waited for some time until at last the man in green pushed back his chair, tossed his drink down his throat and stood up laughing. Sean recognised the laugh at once and the face as it turned merely confirmed that recognition.

''Tis him for sure,' he said.

'Very well,' the Colonel said, drawing deep on his cigar. 'Every battle in my experience has to be planned meticulously. First, children, it has to be said that the rogue may well have sold off your torc already – gold is never difficult to dispose of – and he does have a new suit of fine clothes, gleaming boots and one of the best cabins on the boat. He has money from somewhere.'

'But it could be Little Luke's money that Miss Henry gave him – he stole that too,' Sean said.

'Perhaps, perhaps,' said the Colonel. 'What is certain is that we cannot be certain. Secondly, the torc is in his possession. It belongs to him at present.'

'But he stole it,' Annie said.

'So you say, Annie, so you say. And so I believe. But he would deny it, would he not? In a court of law he would deny it – it would be his word against yours.'

'And Little Luke's,' said Sean.

'Little Luke has gone, and anyway he is black – neither of which would be very useful in a St. Louis courtroom. No, the frontal assault would be of no use. We have either to steal it back, or somehow to winkle it out of him. To steal would be difficult, if not impossible. We do not even know if he has it, let alone where he might be hiding it.' The Colonel paused suddenly in mid-sentence, and behind a screen of cigar smoke the children saw him nodding slowly and then suddenly his face wreathed in a smile of pure delight. The children had never before seen him smile. 'There is a way,' he said, 'but I must have your promise that you will not interfere nor ask questions of me, no matter what happens. Do I have it?' The children nodded without conferring. 'Very well. I will begin my campaign tomorrow. Meanwhile, you will both keep to the wheelhouse and my cabin in case he should recognise you. He may have done so already.'

'Mister Colonel,' said Annie. 'He does not know me at all. 'Twas only half light when he saw us before. I bumped right into him and looked him full in the face – that's how I knew 'twas him – he looked me right in the eyes, Mister Colonel, and he did not know me.'

'In my army, Annie, soldiers do not query an officer's orders,' said the Colonel, with half a smile still in his eyes, 'and from now on you are my soldiers, are you not?'

'Yes, Mister Colonel,' said Annie, who at that moment liked him for the first time.

All that next day both the children watched the Colonel carefully, but he left the wheelhouse only occasionally, so by sundown they were beginning to feel somewhat disappointed. Just the thought that the torc might still be on the boat was so tantalising that neither would allow the other to speak of it.

Then, just before dinner, the Colonel appeared at the door of his cabin with a bottle in his hand, his suit unbuttoned, his hair dishevelled and his face flushed with drink. He brushed past the children, stepped out of the wheelhouse and made his way unsteadily along the upper deck. The man at the helm looked at him astonished and shook his head. Annie took Sean by the arm and they followed him out into the darkness. They saw the saloon door open and the Colonel disappear inside. The rain was sheeting down – but this was refreshing and quite welcome to them for it kept away the clouds of mosquitoes and midges that plagued them each night. They made their way to the same window and crouched down. The gamblers round the table looked on as the Colonel pulled bank notes in handfuls out of his pocket and deposited them in an untidy pile on the table. Then he sat down heavily and lit a cigar. Until then they had neither of them noticed the man in green. He was sitting opposite the Colonel, this time in full view of the children.

'But he's gambling,' said Annie too loudly. 'He said he'd never gamble again. He told us.'

'Not so loud,' Sean whispered. 'Can you not see, Annie? 'Tis his plan. He's going to win back the torc for us. The man's a genius, a genius.'

'But why is he drinking?' Annie asked. 'I've never seen him drinking before.'

'He'll be just pretending,' said Sean, trying to stifle the cough that had been troubling him recently. 'Sure he's just pretending.' And Annie wanted to believe him but could not.

They waited and watched out in the rain, full of expectation. But every game the Colonel played brought disappointment, for the Colonel's pile of notes diminished rapidly as he lost each hand, until there was nothing left. They saw him try to get to his feet, stumble and fall across the table. Annie was on her feet in an instant and was all for running in to help him, but Sean held her back. 'We promised not to interfere,' he said. 'Remember?' And they crept back to their cabin, took off their wet clothes and climbed into bed before the Colonel returned. But he never did, and when the children awoke in the morning they saw his bed had not been slept in. They found him in the wheelhouse, chewing an unlit cigar and sipping coffee. He did not speak to them then, nor in the days that followed.

Every night for a week he would make his way along the deck to the gambling saloon and the children would follow and watch him lose. From time to time it was true the Colonel seemed to regain his composure, drink less and begin to win. But in the darkness outside the children's hopes were raised only to be dashed sooner or later for the recovery was always shortlived. At the end of each night's gambling they would either have to help him back to his cabin or he would shrug them off and would stagger back to the cabin alone. Gone was the elegance and the poise. He was scarcely ever to be seen now without a bottle in his hand. The puritanical German migrants turned away whenever he approached, and his crew shook their heads sadly. Only at the helm and in the running of his boat did the Colonel seem to be as sharp as ever.

The morning of the 4th July saw the *Henry Martha* steaming through a dawn heat-haze that shrouded the river from bank to bank. The Colonel stayed at the wheel until the mist lifted and then he came to sit down at the breakfast table with the children. They did not speak to him – a sullen withdrawal born of resentment and disappointment, but also out of fear that he would bark at them as he had done so often during the last week. Only Sean's hacking cough broke the silence between them. But it was he who spoke to them, and civilly too. 'Don't like the sound of that cough, Sean O'Brien. You'd best stay in the dry.' Sean said nothing. 'You've not a lot of faith in your old Colonel any more, have you, children?' he said sitting back and waiting for them to look up at him. But they did not.

'Miss Henry would be 'shamed of you, Mister Colonel,' said Annie, her voice barely audible.

'That's for sure,' the Colonel admitted.

'And I'm 'shamed of you,' said Annie looking up at him, her eyes full of tears. 'You are 'spicable and I'm not your soldier any more.' And she ran out of the cabin.

'And what about you, Sean?' said the Colonel. 'Are you going to desert me too?'

'No, Colonel,' said Sean sadly. ''Tis never we who have deserted you; 'tis you who have deserted us.'

'Maybe, Sean O'Brien,' the Colonel said considering the end of his cigar. 'Maybe. But don't give me up quite yet. Be sure you're in the saloon this evening – everyone else will be. Be there early or else you won't be able to see. And be sure you bring your little sister even if she doesn't want to come. And Sean, you're to stay in the dry and keep warm. Do you hear me, now?'

Annie first heard the rumour when she was with her friends the German migrants. There was much criticism amongst them of the Colonel's drunkenness and Annie found herself defending him. 'Annie, the Colonel is not safe, he is not safe a ship to command,' said one of their elders. 'But it is said he will not be so for much longer.'

'What d'you mean?' Annie asked.

'It is said he will tonight put the boat as a stake in the poker game. It is said it is all he has left. All the boat speaks of it. Tomorrow we will have a new captain perhaps.'

That evening the saloon was so full that although the children were there by dark they had to crawl through the legs of the crowd to have a clear view of the card table. At every windowpane Sean saw a face peering into the cabin, nose pressed against the steaming glass. The boat was moored that night, and even the jetty was crowded. News had spread into the little township that the *Henry Martha* might be changing hands over the card table, and that was a prospect no one wanted to miss.

CHAPTER 24

THE COLONEL SAT WHITE-FACED, STIFF AND silent at one end of the table; and at the other, surrounded by his noisy cronies, sat the bounty hunter in the green velvet jacket, his face flushed with triumph. All around, bets were being taken on the outcome, the odds heavily against the Colonel, and it was some time before the dealer's call for silence was obeyed. 'Gentlemen,' he said solemnly. 'You have examined the cards. This is straight poker. Colonel Whitman here has stated that he is prepared to put the *Henry Martha* on the table as his stake, providing you, sir, can match it. I have examined the boat and valued it at three thousand dollars – she's not as young as she was, Colonel. I understand you can meet this, sir.'

'Damn right I can,' said the man in green. 'I got two thousand greenbacks, most of it from him, and his notes for three hundred dollars more.' At this there was raucous laughter until the dealer silenced it. 'An' I got the rest in gold.' At this he reached inside his jacket and produced wads of dollars and finally held aloft the golden torc. There was a buzz of astonishment.

'Are you satisfied, Colonel Whitman?' said the dealer.

'I want to see it first, sir,' said the Colonel, and the dealer passed the torc across the table. The Colonel examined it carefully. 'This is not pure gold,' he said after a long silence. 'Pure gold would not spring like this. It's too dull and red. It contains an alloy of some kind, copper I should guess and a considerable percentage of silver. If this is all he has to offer, then I must withdraw.' And the Colonel made to stand up.

'Chicken,' scoffed the bounty hunter. 'The Colonel's chicken. Anyways, I ain't got nothin' else.'

'Sir,' said the Colonel drily. 'A chicken can lay eggs. She helps to feed people. She is of some use in this world. May I ask if you have ever in all your miserable life done anything as useful? You're a fool, sir, a scavenger and a scoundrel.'

The bounty hunter sprang to his feet, a gun suddenly in his hand. Sean recognised it at once as Miss Henry's revolver. He was about to tell Annie, but things moved too fast and anyway he felt from the clasp of her hand on his shoulder that she knew it. 'A liar too, it appears,' said the Colonel quickly. 'You said a moment ago sir, that you had nothing else. You have a gun I see and the clothes you stand up in. If those are part of the stake I shall be satisfied.'

'Well sir,' said the dealer looking up at the bounty hunter whose face was red with fury. 'Will you put the gun away and play the game sir?'

'I will,' he said, sitting down again. 'An' when I've finished with you here, Colonel, I'll take great pleasure in throwin' you off my boat.'

'Everything on this one hand then?' said the dealer, and both the Colonel and the bounty hunter nodded their agreement.

The two children were kneeling right by the table. Annie was only just tall enough to see over the top. Sean found it hard to take his eyes off the torc that rested like a golden coronet on the pile of notes. It was so close he could reach out and touch it. The

Colonel never looked at them once, but took his cards and examined them almost casually. Each time he took one he turned them face down on the table and sat stoney-faced looking at his opponent who was becoming more and more confident with each card he took. Sean hardly dared to look as the bounty hunter laid down his cards triumphantly to reveal four kings and a ten of clubs.

'A good hand,' said the Colonel, nodding his head slowly after the hubbub had died down. 'Too good I fear to be an honest hand, but even if it were honest it would not be enough, sir.' And one by one he laid out four aces and a queen of hearts. 'She's the prettiest card in the pack,' said the Colonel getting to his feet and pushing back his grey jacket to reveal his gun. Mouth open and suddenly ashen-faced, the bounty hunter looked up at him with unbelieving eyes. 'For more than a week, sir,' said the Colonel, 'you have been cheating me. I have cause enough to shoot you like the dog you are. But you are worse than a dog. Some weeks back outside Pittsburg you robbed my two young friends here of everything they had in this world, and that was not much. Ah, I see you remember them now. The gun belongs to them, the torc belongs to them; and the money for your fine clothes you stole from my sisters' servant whom you kidnapped.' The bounty hunter listened, his eyes flicking from the children to the Colonel in disbelief. 'Now, sir, you owe me that green jacket. You will oblige me by removing it and placing it down on the table. You will remove your boots and your trousers and place those on the table too. Then I shall throw you off my ship.'

'Come on,' said the bounty hunter to his cronies behind him. 'You cain't let him do this to me. It's lies, all of it, lies.' But when he saw his friends backing away he shrugged his shoulders and took off his velvet jacket. At gun-point the Colonel marched him out of the saloon and down the companionway to the main deck. There the bounty hunter removed his boots and trousers, and to roars of laughter chose to jump into the murky black waters of the Ohio rather than be thrown in.

The Colonel was immediately surrounded and fêted, but he raised his hands above them to quieten them. 'Some of you good people have not been Americans long enough to know that on the Fourth of July we've got something special to celebrate and this evening we are going to celebrate like we never did before. Sean O'Brien here will play his fiddle and

Annie will dance as only she can. And as for me, I am going to have a drink. And for those of you of little faith and perception who thought I had been drinking a little too much in recent days, I should ask you to remember that this bottle is half full now, the same half full as it was a week ago, but I have a feeling it could be empty by the morning.'

The feasting and the dancing went on well into the night, the entire ship lit up like a great Christmas cake from end to end. Bawdy frontier ballads, German folk tunes and the Irish jigs mingled in discordant unison as the dawn came up over the Ohio River; and the children crawled exhausted into their bed and slept. It was only a few minutes after that the Colonel tiptoed bootless into the cabin. 'You awake, little people?' he whispered. But no one answered. 'Thought not,' he said. He crept over to where the two children lay asleep, the golden torc hanging on a picture hook above them. 'Not bad was I?' he said. 'I mean, considering I haven't been on the stage since I was a boy and considering I haven't gambled nigh on thirty years. Hadn't lost the old magic, had I? Thought I performed fairly well. I go to bed, little people, not a little inebriated and not a little happy.'

'You cheated,' said Annie, rising up on her elbows. 'I saw you under the table. I saw where that ace of diamonds came from.'

'Well, that's gratitude for you,' said the Colonel. 'Of course I cheated, Annie. I cheated because he cheated. I just did it better, that's all. Did you see where the ace of hearts came from? You didn't, did you? Masterly it was, masterly. What did you want me to do, lose? And anyway you got back your golden torc, or whatever you call it, Sean has his gun and the world's righted itself, so what are you grumbling about, young lady?'

'I'm never grumbling, Mister Colonel. I just wanted you to know that I knew, that's all. An' I want you to know we're terrible 'shamed we ever doubted you, isn't that right, Sean?'

'I never did,' said Sean into the pillow. He expected an onslaught from his sister and it duly came. He sought refuge under the pillows but to no avail. It took the Colonel some time to pull Annie off him.

'Peace, little people,' he said. 'It's the greatest compliment to me that you believed in my performance. I'm flattered and I'm tired, so go to sleep now.' Some minutes later, stretched out on his bed, he spoke once more. 'You think my sister

Henry would have been proud of me today, little people?' But there was no reply and in the darkness he indeed could hear their breathing, regular and deep and peaceful, punctuated by Sean's persistent coughing. 'Yes, I think perhaps she'd be quite pleased with her little brother, if she ever got to know. I should like her to know, one day perhaps.' And his breathing fell in with theirs and he slept like a child, still smiling.

That was to be the last night of good sleep for Sean. Their nightly vigil outside the saloon in the rain had taken its toll on his health. The cough that had seemed quite ordinary at first worsened and he soon found his breathing tight and rasping. In time the cough settled on his chest and then fever took him over.

The Colonel insisted he stayed in bed, that he could steer a good course without him. But Sean refused to stay alone in the cabin for long and would emerge dark-eyed and frail to stand beside the Colonel at the wheel. A sharp watch had to be kept in the muddied, eddying water for dead trees and embedded flotsam that might threaten the boat. So Sean tried to concentrate on the river ahead. He felt it was his duty to be there for he had seen how worried the Colonel was at the wheel and knew that another pair of eyes was always useful.

Annie was not much concerned about his health at first. She grumbled that his coughing kept her awake at night, and showed him little sympathy. After all, he was up and about and was still eating quite heartily. It was only when he fainted that afternoon in the wheelhouse that she realised at last that something was indeed seriously wrong. Amongst Annie's German migrant friends with whom she now spent almost all her time, was a young doctor and his family; and he it was who was called in to examine Sean. 'The boy is sick,' he announced, 'very sick. He has the pneumonia and it is, I think, advanced. He should at all times be kept warm. He has the fever and he must have water, much water. He may die, he may not. It is in the hands of God.'

'Die?' said Annie. 'But he cannot die, not Sean, not now. He must not. He was fine 'til now. He just had a cough, a cough – that's all there was.'

Annie sat by his bed that day and every day after that. For much of the time, Sean hovered between consciousness and oblivion, unable to separate the real presence of Annie and the Colonel from his dreams. There were days at the beginning when he was lucid and recalled vividly their home in Ireland

and Will and Fiddler Donnelly. But he spoke mostly about Mother and Danny and Mary and little Joe, and in such a way that Annie felt he was preparing to see them once again. But as the boat neared St. Louis and the days passed, his words became disjointed and at last quite beyond understanding. The doctor came several times each day to see him but could now offer no hope for recovery.

Once docked at St. Louis, the Colonel sent for several doctors, but each one was as gloomy as the one before, and when Annie returned to the cabin one evening after a walk around the empty boat, she found the black-robed figure of a priest standing over her brother. 'It is the finish, Annie,' said the Colonel, putting his arm around her. 'I had to send for a priest. He's hardly breathing now.' Fatigue and the growing inevitability of Sean's dying had combined to soften the blow for Annie. She could not grieve yet, for he was still alive, and the drama of his dying was one she had been through before and there had been no tears then, only a sense that a piece of her was dying too. The Colonel led her out of the cabin while the priest performed the Last Rites, a familiar enough ceremony for Annie, but one she never thought to hear said over Sean.

'I'll be the only one now, Mister Colonel,' she said. 'The only one left.'

'Come in,' called the priest, 'come in. I think the boy's trying to say something but I can't understand him.' Sean was wide awake now and whispering through cracked lips, his hand raised and pointing upwards.

'The torc,' said Annie. 'He wants the torc.' And she took it down off the picture hook and put it carefully in his hands, wrapping his fingers around it to be sure he could feel it. He seemed immediately to relax and took away one of his hands and laid it on hers. She stayed with him then and tried to make him drink by moistening his lips gently. As the evening drew on Sean's hand seemed to clasp hers tighter and tighter so that even if she had wanted to take it away she would now find it difficult. Several times the Colonel tried to take her away from him but she would not leave. So long as he was breathing she would not leave him. 'It won't be long now,' she said. 'I've seen it before and I know it won't be long. And Sean was never one to hurry, Mister Colonel, was he? He always thinks hard about what he does before he does it. I think perhaps he's thinking hard just now.'

CHAPTER 25

ANNIE WAS SO CLOSE TO WAKING THAT SHE knew she was dreaming. She was forcing herself back into sleep in order to continue her dream for it needed to be finished and the waking would entirely spoil it. They had found Father's valley in California, a long green valley nestling below the mountains; and there was a silver river curling through it. Father was sitting astride the roof of the house, a hammer in his hand, waving down at them, and they were running through the long grass and Sean was calling out to her. 'Come on, Annie. It's him, it's him.' And he was pulling her by the hand, and she was running so fast to keep up with him that she fell and hit her head against a rock, and Sean was by her side shaking her, trying to wake her, but somehow she didn't want to be woken.

'Annie, wake up, wake up,' said Sean, who was sitting up in bed and shaking her by the shoulder. 'I'm thirsty, Annie,' he said. 'Would you fetch me some water? What's the matter, Annie? You look terrible sick. And the torc must have fallen off the wall for I found it on the bed when I woke just now. Best put it back, Annie – 'tis awful delicate. And what are you looking at me like that for? I ask for a glass of water and you stare at me like I was a ghost or something.'

Annie's shriek of joy was heard all over the riverboat and far beyond on the quayside. The Colonel came hurrying through the door of the cabin. 'Colonel,' said Sean, 'she's squeezing the very life out of me. She's squeezing me dead and all I asked for was a drink of water.'

The Colonel prised Annie away at last and settled Sean back on his pillows. 'We thought we'd lost you, Sean,' he said, trying to excuse his tears. 'It appears the Good Lord decided otherwise, and I'm bound to say I think he made a wise decision.'

Annie had the torc in her hands and gazed at it

reverently before she hung it up over the bed again. 'Don't you 'member, Mister Colonel?' she said. 'Don't you 'member this was the last thing he asked for. The priest had given up, the doctors had given up. We'd all given up and then he asked for the torc.'

'Was it that close?' said Sean, his voice thin and weak. 'Did I nearly die, then?'

'Within a whisker, I should say,' said the Colonel.

The doctor returned that day and the days following and each time he came he whistled through his teeth in sheer disbelief at Sean's miraculous recovery. And every day, the priest came to kneel down by the bed and give thanks for Sean's deliverance. 'The power of prayer,' he would say knowingly as he left them. 'The power of prayer.'

'Sure 'tis nothing of the kind,' said Annie bluntly, when he had gone out. 'I was praying all week was I not, and nothing happened, nothing at all. It was the torc, I tell you. It happened when he touched the torc. Father said he was once told when he was a boy that it had the power of healing, do you not remember that, Sean?'

'I do,' said Sean. 'But I never really believed that, not until now. And even now I'm not sure.'

'Fanciful stuff, children,' said the Colonel

impatiently. 'Smacks of witchery to me. Such imaginings are dangerous to young minds. I'll hear no more of it. Sean needs his rest now, Annie. The doctor says he'll need at least two months to regain his strength, and looking at him I believe the doctor. There's nothing of you, Sean O'Brien, and your face is the colour of the sheets. Only once you're better, once you've rested the winter through, then we shall go out West together and find your father.'

'Together, Mister Colonel?' said Annie. 'Will you be coming with us?'

'I'll be coming too, Annie,' the Colonel said, standing up. 'You've come to be known hereabouts as "the Colonel's children"; and so you are. What would they think of me now if I sent you out into that wilderness all on your own, eh? I began to think about it when you were at death's door, Sean. I determined then that I would deliver Annie personally to her father in Grass Valley, California. And your extraordinary recovery has not altered my mind. If anything it has demonstrated to me what fragile beings we are and how unthinkable it would be for me to allow two children to go all alone out into that terrible wilderness. I know Henry and Martha would never forgive me if anything happened to either of you, and I have already piled up enough misery for my dear sisters without further adding to it. Anyhow, children, I have always yearned to see the Pacific Ocean before I die. They tell me it is there, but I want to find out for myself.'

'What about the river-boat, Mister Colonel?' Annie asked. 'What will happen to the *Henry Martha*?'

'I shall sell her, in the spring. We shall spend the winter months painting her up to look bright and new from bow to stern. But first things first. Whether it was God or the torc – perhaps it was both – that was responsible for your return to the land of the living, they will both now expect you to help yourself. You will eat three good meals a day, stay warm in bed and sleep until you are fully restored – and those are my orders!'

Under the Colonel's firm and careful eye, the climb back to health was slow but sure. The colour crept back into Sean's face and the sunken eyes lost their death shadows. Annie clucked around him like a worried hen, seeing to his every need. Only the prospect of losing her brother had brought home to her how much she cared for him. The role of a loving sister was not one Sean had seen in her before and he loved her for it.

By Christmas that year, Sean was on his feet and well enough to play his fiddle once more. The jigs and reels came back to him easily, and the agility lying dormant in his fingers returned instinctively. Annie's singing and dancing that Christmas evening was not only to please the Colonel, but was by way of a hymn of thanksgiving to whatever power had given her back her brother. She wore the moon-shawl and the torc as she had done the year before in Boston, and the Colonel sat deep in his velvet armchair clapping out the rhythm on his knee, banging with his cane on the floor, and laughing and blowing great smoke rings into the air in time to the music. He proposed a toast to everyone they knew, to Martha, Henry, Little Luke and Bessie, and at the last to all their absent friends. Then he sank back into the chair and beckoned the children to his knees.

'Tomorrow we shall begin to repaint the *Henry Martha*,' he said. 'Will my soldiers follow me into battle with paint brushes at the ready?'

'Anywhere, Mister Colonel,' they said, and they meant it.

*　*　*

But the Colonel grew sad and silent as the work on the river-boat progressed. They would watch him walking alone on the decks after the day's work, the cane tucked under his arm, his hands deep in his pockets unless he took them out to pat and caress the new paintwork. The children tried all they could to lift his spirits, but they knew he was feeling the parting already.

'Been my wife for the last twelve years,' he said, when they at last finished the work. 'Looks better now than when we first got married, and that's thanks to you children – couldn't have done it without you. Makes me proud to look at her all gleaming and bright. Finest-looking boat on the Missouri, she always was and she always will be. She'll fetch a handsome price.' The children both sensed the regret in his voice, but only Annie spoke out.

'You don't have to come with us, Mister Colonel,' she said. 'Sean's well again now. We could manage.'

'No, I don't have to come with you, Annie,' said the Colonel putting his arm around her. 'I want to come with you. In my life I have not often done the right thing. I'm doing it now, not just because I know I should do it, but because I want to do it. Unfortunately, that doesn't make it any easier to part with the old *Henry Martha*. I'm a jealous old coot. Sometimes I think I would rather steam out into mid-channel and scuttle her than let someone else have her. But that would be like murder, couldn't do it. The old girl's got a lot of life in her yet. She has a sound heart; engine and paddles turn as smooth as silk. Besides, children, where else are we going to get enough money to buy our wagons, our supplies and a good team of mules? And what am I going to do in California without any money? A man needs money to live on almost as much as he needs water. Fact of life, children, fact of life.'

CHAPTER 26

AND SO IT WAS THAT IN EARLY APRIL, THE *HENRY Martha* steamed out of St. Louis up-river for Independence with a new Captain at the wheel, a young Dutchman more used to the canals of Amsterdam, who had paid five thousand dollars for her. And amongst the crowds of migrants jamming the decks were the Colonel and his two children camped out on the deck in their new farm wagon. Below in the hold was the team of four mules that the Colonel had picked out in St. Louis. The *Henry Martha* was fully laden and lay low in the water. The Colonel said she was too low in the water for comfort, but battling against the swirling currents she fought her way up the Missouri steering an erratic course and grating on sandbars as she went.

The Colonel fumed in his wagon all that first day at the poor navigation, and at last he could bear it no longer. 'Our new Captain needs a lesson,' he said, throwing away his cigar. 'The *Henry Martha* deserves better than this and she's going to get it.' And he disappeared into the wheelhouse. From then on until they reached Independence a week later the river-boat steered a perfect course, and everyone on board knew why.

For the migrants the journey up the Missouri was a great fiesta. There was all about a feeling of great optimism and release. Many had travelled overland for hundreds of miles and were already exhausted, but even these felt a new surge of excitement, for the great trek west was at last under way. By days the children made the decks their playground and the boat echoed to their shrieks and whoops of delight; and by nights Sean brought out his fiddle and the river-boat fairly danced on the water. The wagons, hooped and canvassed, were piled high with every kind of household furniture, from washtubs to grandfather clocks; there were ploughs and chicken coops, and sacks of barley and wheat. Most of the migrants were farmers from the east, seeking to carve out farms from the virgin wilderness of Oregon or California. A few were French, and these carried their precious vines with them that they would replant in the sunshine of California. There were the trappers and mountain men who kept apart from the migrants, and here and there, groups of Indians with smooth shaved heads and grimly-painted faces, wrapped in strange flowing robes that whipped about them in the wind. Sean and Annie had seen Indians before of course, but never in such numbers. They too kept themselves apart from the migrants, camping together in one corner of the upper deck.

The children had strict instructions never to leave the wagons unguarded. Sean had been detailed to see to the mules below, so that Annie was often left to guard the wagon alone. She would sit at the rear of the wagon in the Colonel's red velvet chair, the fiddle case across her knees. Behind her was the Colonel's trunk into which he had packed all his worldly goods and theirs. But Annie was content enough for she was able to combine her sentry duties with making friends. Soon the grand velvet chair became known as 'Queen Annie's throne', and it was always surrounded with happy, laughing children who came to call on their queen and rarely went away – much to Sean's dismay.

But the mood of euphoria ended abruptly when they docked at Independence, a straggling, bustling town of blacksmiths, wheelrights and saddlers that teemed with migrants making their last preparations before they moved out to the great camps on the prairies beyond, where the wagons gathered before 'jump-off'.

With scarcely a glance over his shoulders the Colonel left his beloved *Henry Martha* behind him and drove the wagon determinedly through the chaos, with Sean and Annie sitting beside him. By nightfall they had reached the edge of the prairies and as they came out of the trees, saw below them a circle of camp fires glittering in the dusk.

'Well, children,' said the Colonel, pulling up the mules. 'It appears we shall not be short of company on our journey. The difficulty will be, I think, in finding the right company. Two thousand miles is a long way to travel together – a man must be sure of his friends.'

They camped that night some distance from the circle of wagons. They received several visits as they sat eating their supper over the fire. Many came just to look and go away again, but others stayed to talk, particularly the children. They were all farmers, it seemed, mostly from Pennsylvania and Illinois going to California. A few had come up from St. Louis on the *Henry Martha* and they knew them already – Annie was reunited with many of her little friends – and it was one of these farmers that invited them that evening to a meeting.

The meeting was held around a great crackling fire in the centre of the circle of wagons. It was already in progress by the time the Colonel arrived with Sean and Annie, and already it was vociferous and bitter. There were accusations and counter-accusations, angry pointing fingers and shaking fists. It seemed they were trying to decide who should be elected Captain of the wagon-train and what rules should govern them on their journey. Almost everyone was a candidate for Captain and everyone had a notion about what rules there should or should not be. Two hours later they were still arguing ferociously.

The Colonel said nothing, but sat silent, puffing from time to time on his cigar. Sitting next to him, Sean could feel his simmering frustration. At last the Colonel could bear it no longer, threw his cigar to the ground, rose to his feet and limped out into the light of the fire. He held up his cane for silence and did not begin to speak until every voice was hushed.

'My name is Colonel Whitman,' he said. 'Colonel Paul Whitman. I was invited to come to this meeting, but that is hardly what it can be called. More like a cock fight, not a sport I'm fond of. I understand that you are seeking someone to lead the wagons across to California. I have been thinking it over and will be willing to offer my services.'

'Why you?' someone called out.

'Well to begin with, sir, you seem incapable of choosing anyone else. Secondly, sir, you are all farmers. You know your land, you know your stock, you can read the weather from the wind, from the clouds. You know when to plough and when to till. I can do none of those things, but I am, or was, a soldier. My business was to lead men into danger and bring them through it. More recently, as some of you will know, I was Captain of the river-boat, the *Henry Martha*. I have to tell you that as a soldier I never lost a battle and as a ship's Captain I never lost a ship, although I came close to both. Those are my qualifications, sir, for what they are worth.'

'We need a younger man,' someone else shouted,

and there was a chorus of agreement.

'We need younger men to drive the wagons, and the stock, to forage, to hunt and scout,' said the Colonel. 'Every one of you here, man, woman and child, has his part to play if we are going to reach California before winter, and reach it we must, or perish. Ahead of us lies two thousand miles of some of the worst territory on earth – scorching plains, flooding rivers, Indians, wolves, deserts and the cold high sierras. I will get you there if you will let me. But I will hide nothing from you. I shall be a hard task-master. As your leader I will have to make harsh decisions on your behalf. Some you will not approve of; some you will not like. Therefore I must have your absolute trust from the outset. To argue on the way, to dispute every order could prove fatal to all of us. If I am to lead you I must be given the power to make the rules, to punish, to appoint and to dismiss. I know no other way to command. You cannot expect to like me if you vote for me, but you can expect to reach California – alive.'

'That's straight talkin', Colonel, and I like a man that talks straight,' said a voice from the shadows. The man it belonged to stepped up to him and shook his hand. 'I'm Matt Colby, Colonel, farmer from

Illinois, and I surely liked what I heard. You get my vote, that's for sure.' And he turned and spoke to everyone. 'Friends, we got all the wagons we need to start. We don't need no more. We bin arguing here for days, and this man spoke the first sense I heard. Now I got me twenty head of cattle and a family to feed on this journey. I wanna be first on the trail this spring, first to the grazing, first to every water hole. I don't want the prairies eaten and hunted out in front of us so there's nothing left for us when we come along. And that's what will happen if we sit about here arguing. I don't wanna eat no man's dust for two thousand miles. I say this man's the fittest person here to lead us. And I say we puts our trust in him and makes him our Captain.'

Not a single vote was counted against the Colonel and they clapped and cheered him till he called again for silence. 'I thank you for your confidence, friends,' he said. 'And I aim to repay that confidence. I agree with Mr Colby here. There's wagons by the hundred back in Independence and they'll be coming this way soon as they're ready. We should leave at dawn tomorrow if we are to keep ahead of them. I noticed when I came into the camp that there were no sentries posted. From now on I want sentries posted at every fourth wagon, Mr Colby. Perhaps you'll see to it. Tomorrow when we leave I want two tight lines of wagons. No stragglers. If you've got a problem with a wheel or a shaft, you let the out-riders know and they'll tell me. We'll be leaving no one behind. The Pawnees are quiet at present, but any stragglers would tempt them and we don't want to do that, do we now? We shall want three men to ride on ahead with the guide and two to bring up the rear – not a pleasant job but we'll all take our turn – and I want out-riders on each flank. We do have a guide I hope, Mr Colby?'

'Charlie Charbonnier,' said Matt Colby, 'French Charlie they call him. Said he'd be back at dawn, Colonel. He's in Independence saying goodbye to his friends, has been for 'bout three days now.'

'Well, you send him to me as soon as he gets in,' said the Colonel. 'Let's start right now with a few simple rules for everyone's safety. No one leaves the camp alone at night, and no one goes unarmed outside the perimeter of the corral. And no alcohol, gentlemen, water is fine when we can find it – at times it will be scarce enough – but there'll be no whiskey drunk on this wagon-train.'

'French Charlie won't like that,' said someone.

'None of us will like it,' said the Colonel. 'I don't like it. But guns and whiskey don't mix easily at the best of times. Whiskey saps a man and we shall need all our strength if we are to reach California. Remember this, friends, there will be hard times ahead for everyone. We have to live through them together or we shan't live at all. Now goodnight to you all, and sleep well. We have an early start tomorrow.'

In the wagon that night, Sean and Annie lay side by side under their blankets and watched the Colonel sitting back in his chair and blowing his smoke rings out into the starlit sky. He was looking up at the stars. 'Always a source of wonderment to me, children, that up there somewhere could be an old Colonel lying back in his chair and puffing on his cigar and looking right up at us and saying to his children, "always a source of wonderment to me, children, that up there somewhere could be an old Colonel lying back in his chair, puffing at his cigar . . ." '

Annie interrupted him. 'But that could go on for ever,' she said, laughing.

'Course it could,' said the Colonel. 'It's a lullaby my mother used to tell me. It's like counting sheep – it sends you to sleep.'

'Do you think maybe Father could be looking up at those same stars and thinking of us?' Sean asked.

'I hope so, Sean,' said the Colonel. 'I hope so.'

'Well, I know so,' Annie said. 'He'll be waiting for us in Grass Valley. I know he will.'

CHAPTER 27

AS DAYLIGHT SPREAD ON TO THE PRAIRIE AND silenced the whistling quails and the whippoorwills, the men stumbled out of their wagons to breakfast and then to harness their stock. There was a cacophony of cursing and shouting, braying and neighing and lowing. Horses and mules bolted in all directions and oxen obstinately refused to move. Barking dogs stampeded the cattle and then rounded them up only to drive them in the wrong direction. Through the confusion the Colonel sat grim-faced on the seat of his wagon, Sean holding the reins by his side.

'Seems like we got a lot to learn, Matt,' said the Colonel dryly as Matt Colby rode up to the wagon accompanied by a man in a coonskin hat who rode his horse as if it were a part of him.

'They'll settle down, Colonel,' said Matt. 'For some of those teams it's the first time in harness. They'll settle down. I brought French Charlie to see you, like you said.'

'Now see here, Colonel,' said French Charlie, dismounting beside the wagon. He was a young man, lithe and springing as he jumped down, but his face was the brown of leather and creased old by the elements. He wore a thick red flannel shirt that was open at the neck. 'Now see here. I hear tell you said there's to be no drinkin' of whiskey on this train. They tell me I had a French father but I've a Scots mother and I've had whiskey in my blood since the day I was born and before that. I'll not be told by no army Colonel when I can and cannot drink. Understand?'

'Perfectly, Mr Charbonnier,' said the Colonel stiffly. 'But answer me a few questions if you please. Are you employed by the people of this wagon-train to guide them to California?'

'I am.'

'Good. Now will you do the job better drunk or sober?' The Colonel paused. 'I see you do not answer,

Mr Charbonnier. You will therefore understand why I can allow no drink whilst we are on the trail. Now understanding that, and understanding that I am the Captain of this train and you will do as I say, will you take the job or return to Independence?'

The man's anger seemed to ebb as he took time to think. Then he nodded slowly, an unpleasant smile curling his lips. 'I have taken out a train last year all the way to California, Colonel,' he said quietly. 'We had three wagon captains before we reached California. You'll understand soon enough, Colonel, that these people need me more than you. But you're the boss for now and I can do without my whiskey.'

'That's good enough for me, Mr Charbonnier,' said the Colonel. 'I'm glad we understand one another. Now these are my orders. You will ride not less than one mile ahead of the column with three scouts. I shall be in the lead wagon. You will report back to me any problems – sightings of Indians, river crossings – send back one of the scouts. I calculate we should be travelling at about fifteen to twenty miles a day, all being well.'

'You'll be lucky, Colonel,' said French Charlie, swinging up into his saddle. 'You'll be lucky.'

'I hope so, Mr Charbonnier,' said the Colonel. 'I hope so, for all our sakes.'

'I don't trust that man,' said Annie when he had gone. 'He has a terrible wicked look to his face.'

'Maybe,' said the Colonel. 'But he's the only guide we have, so we'd best make what we can of him. Send out the scouts, Mr Colby, and have the wagons roll. We have a hell of a way to go.' As Mr Colby gave the word, Sean sweetened the mules into a walk and the wagon train plodded out across the stream below them and out on to the open prairie, a sea of rolling green hills that stretched away in front of them, the long grass whipped by the wind into undulating waves. Ahead of him he could see French Charlie and the scouts spurring their horses over the first rise until they were lost from sight. Looking behind her, Annie watched the wagons rocking along in two straggling lines and on either side the out-riders rounding up the cattle, whooping and yelling at any beast that had the temerity to break ranks.

'There's sixty wagons behind us, Mister Colonel,' Annie said. 'I counted them and they're all coming. We're all moving, Mister Colonel. We're on our way, we're on our way.'

The first day was a sweet spring day with only a

few wisps of cloud marring a clear blue sky. Larks rose shrill above them and they came across stream after stream where the fording was easy and where the animals could water and the migrants could wash the dust off. The hills about them were lush with myriads of wild flowers that Annie picked whenever she could to decorate the inside of the wagon. There were a few more idyllic days like this as the train settled into its slow plodding rhythm, and every new day the draft-animals bent to their task more willingly. Sean drove the mules as Little Luke had taught him back in Boston, with the reins tight and in touch always with the mules' mouths. He it was who set the pace for the entire train. The nights were sultry and scented and they were lulled to sleep by a thousand frog songs and humming, chirruping insects. But the honeymoon was not to last for long.

CHAPTER 28

IT WAS DURING A MIDDAY STOP THAT THE farmers first smelt damp in the wind that warned them of an approaching storm. That afternoon the sky darkened overhead and the very earth seemed to shake beneath them. The Colonel corralled the wagons just before the rain came. Driven by a terrible wind it fell in unremitting torrents. It pounded through the canvas on the wagons and drenched man and beast alike. As night fell, lightning flashed across the prairie and the cattle broke in fear and scattered into the hills; teams of oxen and mules reared and plunged and bolted in blind terror. It lasted all night long and by morning there was a scene of utter ruin and despair. It took fully two days to recover the stock and repair the damage before they could move on again.

Now, of course, there was mud to contend with and where before the ground had been firm and easy, it turned into a quagmire. The wagons sank to the axle and stuck and had to be man-handled out on to the hard ground. The streams were swollen and could no longer be easily forded. Five wagons had to be abandoned and three families turned back in despair. Several mules and horses were tethered badly at night and ran away, never to be found again. The Colonel gave the order that all horses and mules were to be hobbled from now on, but that could not bring the lost ones back. They had barely gone one hundred miles. And worse was to come.

As they left the gentle hills of Kansas behind them, they reached the Platte River and the wide open prairie with scarcely a tree in sight. The buffalo, deer and elk that had fed them since their journey began could no longer be found so easily and the forragers and hunters often came home empty-handed. Like everyone else, Sean and Annie had to live on biscuits and salt beef. They passed pale skeletons of buffalo that mocked them, and many of the springs and waterholes were so foul that they could not be used. At night they fought the mosquitoes and tried to forget the howling of the wolves outside the corral of wagons – they were too close to let sleep come easily. There was now no longer any wood even to build the fires. Fights broke out over what there was left and many times the Colonel had physically to separate the antagonists. There was only the fuzz of cottonwood that burned out quickly, and buffalo dung, when it could be found. This they used for cooking whenever they could, but there was not enough of it and in the incessant wind it burned out always too quickly.

By now, discontent was rife among the farmers. Every setback was blamed on the Colonel. The disappointment felt at each polluted waterhole was turned against the Colonel. Annie spent much of her time in the other wagons with her friends and she heard the whispers and spoke out against them, but to no avail. It was down to bad leadership, they said. Someone should have warned them. Someone should have told them what it would be like. The Colonel did not know what he was doing. Only Matt Colby and a few of the farmers remained constant and loyal to the Colonel. Through it all the Colonel remained cheerful, lending a sympathetic ear whenever it was needed. He sat in judgement over the squabbles and became adept at smoothing ruffled pride before it flared into violence. But when camp fever set in as they neared Fort Laramie and many of the children became ill, the complaints finally came out into the open. The farmers sent a delegation to the Colonel to ask him to stop, but the Colonel was adamant. They would rest, he said, only when they reached Fort Laramie. Provisions were running short, water was short. They had to press on. Now Sean and Annie heard vicious murmurings against the Colonel amongst their friends, but neither said anything to the Colonel for they knew it would hurt him to know how much they had come to hate him.

It was after one of the sick children died that Sean could stand the taunting no longer. He was tuning his fiddle shortly after they had come to rest for the night when one of the farmer's sons, who had been spoiling for a fight with him, approached the wagon. The Colonel was with Matt Colby checking the horses down by the stream. 'I come to say your Colonel's a lousy murderer, Sean O'Brien,' said the boy, who towered inches over Sean. 'If we'd have stopped back there like my pa said, that child'd be living right now. He's a lousy murderer.'

Sean rose to his feet slowly and handed the fiddle to Annie who tried to hold him back. But Sean shook himself free and launched himself at the boy. They rolled in the dust kicking and punching and a crowd began to gather from all over the camp. In no time at all they were surrounded by screaming children baying for blood. And blood there was. Before he was finished Sean had split the boy's lip and suffered a torn ear himself, and they only finished because the Colonel was pulling them apart and shaking them to their senses. 'And what's it all about, Sean?' said the Colonel. By this time everyone on the wagon-train, it seemed, had arrived for the spectacle.

'He was calling you a murderer, Colonel,' said Sean, fighting to regain his breath. 'Sure they blame you for everything that goes wrong.'

'That was kind of you, Sean,' said the Colonel. 'But words are not worth fighting for.' And he lifted his voice and spoke to everyone. 'I told you all before we embarked on this journey that you wouldn't like some of the decisions I had to make. I am sorry the child died, but more of us will die if we fight amongst each other. The scouts have just come back and told me that we'll be in Fort Laramie by tomorrow afternoon. There we can rest for a few days. But there'll be worse to come after that. I'm not a god, and I can't make it easy for you. That's all I have to say. Now get back to your wagons and leave me to mine.'

Later that evening, as Annie was bathing Sean's ear, the Colonel came in from his rounds. He had been limping worse of late and he held his leg and winced as he sat down heavily in his chair. 'Old wound's playing me up. You don't think me a cruel man, children, do you?' he said.

'Mister Colonel,' said Annie, bending over to kiss him on the cheek, 'it does not matter what they think out there. We know why you came on this journey and we know how hard it must be for you. They'll be happy enough soon as we reach the Fort, soon as there's plenty of water and plenty of food.'

'I hope so,' said the Colonel. 'I hope you're right.'

And sure enough Fort Laramie proved a tonic to everyone. Here for the first time, their bruised bodies could rest, they could wash their clothes and restock with supplies. Wheels shrunken in the sun were relined with steel and torn canvasses replaced. Oxen were thrown on their backs in deep trenches to be reshod, and the horses' and mules' feet trimmed and shoed. Slowly the weary migrants regained their spirits and surly farmers smiled once again at Sean and Annie as they passed.

On the last night at Fort Laramie an ox was roasted and a great feast was held. They danced and sang to Sean's fiddle and drank deep until at midnight the Colonel called a halt to the festivities. 'To your beds, my friends,' he said. 'We have deserts and mountains ahead of us before we reach California. We have done well, my friends. We have suffered together and come through thus far. I cannot tell you what lies ahead. Only do not lose faith in the weeks to come. I'll do all I can – I can do no more. See that the water barrels are filled to the brim, Mr Colby. We shall be needing every drop.' Some of them still cheered him that night, but Sean and Annie noticed that many did not.

It was at that party that Annie saw a huddle of farmers muttering to each other. One of them was a weasley-looking roustabout with a black beard who glared horribly at the children whenever they came across each other. From the minute she first saw him Annie knew she had seen him somewhere before, and night after night on the trail she had racked her memory, trying to place the man behind the beard, but she could not. French Charlie was in amongst them and appeared to be their leader. They did not join in the dancing and ignored the Colonel while he was speaking. She confided her suspicions to Sean, that they might be up to no good; and they told the Colonel, but the Colonel dismissed the idea.

'This is a country of free men,' he said. 'I do not like French Charlie any more than you do, but I cannot stop him talking to people.'

It was many weeks later, as they crawled up towards the Blackrock Desert, that the murmurings of mutiny were heard once more. The crossing of the desert was enough to destroy men and animals at the peak of health and stamina, for not a drop of water was to be had for fifty miles or more until they reached the other side. Dejected and demoralised, the wagons struggled on. The cattle that could move no further had to be left to die. Clocks, tables and chairs littered the path behind them as the Colonel ordered them to lighten the load for the oxen and mules. Reluctantly, the Colonel himself toppled his beloved velvet armchair out of the wagon to encourage the others. He drove them on remorselessly. He stomached no excuses and no delays.

It was at the water-butt one blazing August morning before the wagon-train moved off, that the rumbling mutiny first flared briefly into the open. The Colonel, with Annie and Sean beside him, was giving out the water ration to each family when French Charlie came back for more. 'I work harder than the others, Colonel, and I'll have some more water, if you please,' he said deliberately loudly so that everyone could hear.

The Colonel ignored him at first and then as quick as lightning there was a gun in his hand. 'Mr Charbonnier,' he said, 'if you take more water that means less for someone else, and none for someone else. If you force me to shoot you, I will. No one will have more than his ration. We will survive only if we all share. Everyone must have an equal share, Mr Charbonnier, no matter how important they are.' The two men looked at each other for a full minute and the farmers all around gathered their children and backed away towards the wagons. French Charlie turned on his heel and walked away.

It was the next morning, before dawn, that the Colonel woke to see a rifle barrel pointing between his eyes, and a triumphant French Charlie grinning down at him. With the Colonel, Sean and Annie were dragged out into the open. The wagon was completely surrounded with men carrying rifles. It was one of these that strode up to the Colonel. 'I bin meanin' to catch up with you, Colonel.' Annie at once recognised the voice, although she could not make out the face under the hat. 'Remember our little game of cards, Colonel? Well, Colonel, seems you lost after all, don't it?' And he turned and came across to the children. 'Well, lookee who's here. Don't you recognise your old friend from way back? I can see you do, little girl, I can see you do. I grewed this beard special, just for you, 'cos I knew we'd be meeting up one day. Now I got a nice surprise for you. French Charlie here wanted to kill you all, but I said no, that ain't right, we'll just leave 'em out here in the middle of nowhere without a drop of water, and 'cos French Charlie's an obligin' sort, he agreed with me. Now ain't that just fine? Course, 'fore we leave you; I'd be obliged if you'd open up that fiddle case of your'n and hand me that gold necklet you stole from me all that while ago.'

CHAPTER 29

AS THE UNWELCOME SUN CAME UP AGAIN OVER the desert, the wagon-train began to leave. The Colonel sat on the ground by the shafts of the wagon, his arm around Annie's shoulder. Sean stood above them, fiercely protective of the Colonel in his humiliation. Every jibe and insult hurled at the Colonel from the passing wagons received a vociferous response from Sean. But the Colonel sat silent as the bounty hunter taunted him, dangling the torc in front of his face. 'You'll have to kill me to get this off me again, soldier boy,' he said. 'An' you ain't about to do that, is you, soldier boy? A man dries out slowly in the sun,' and the man smiled a hideous smile. 'It'll be a slow death. 'Fraid we ain't got no water to spare you, soldier boy.'

All around them, the farmers were hitching up their horses and piling their families into the wagons. Most of them ignored the Colonel and his children. After the initial excitement over the success of the mutiny, and the issuing of unlimited rations of water, a kind of guilty resignation had set in about the treatment of the Colonel. One or two farmers, Matt Colby amongst them, pleaded for the Colonel to be taken along, but no one paid them any heed. A few of Annie's friends, and she had precious few left now, tried to talk to her, but they were always hurried away by fearful parents, none of whom would even look at the Colonel. When one of Annie's friends lifted her hand to wave at Annie as she passed by, her mother slapped her hand and bustled her away.

French Charlie rode up, tall on his horse, and there was a swagger in his voice as he looked down at the Colonel. 'I warned you, Colonel,' he said. 'Right from the start I warned you. But you wouldn't listen. No sir, you always knew best. See, they know I'm the only one who knows the way out of this wilderness. I'm the one they need, Colonel.' And then he turned to Sean and Annie who glowered at him. 'You two can come along in Matt Colby's wagon – says he's got room for you.'

'We'll not be leaving the Colonel,' said Sean. 'We'll be staying here where we belong.'

'I ain't got the time to argue, son,' said French Charlie. 'But you gotta know that if you stay here you'll die 'long with the Colonel. We taken your mules 'cos we needed 'em, and we ain't leavin' the Colonel no water. We ain't got none to spare. There ain't no way you gonna get out of this desert if you stay. Sun'll burn you up inside twenty-four hours.'

Annie was on her feet screaming at him. 'We got more chance here with the Colonel, Mister, than you've got without him. 'Sides the Colonel's our friend and we'll never leave him, not ever.'

'Leave 'em be, Charlie,' said the bounty hunter, mounting his horse. 'They ain't worth the bother. They wanna stay out here in the desert an' die, let 'em stay.'

'Mister,' said Annie, squeezing her eyes tight against the glare of the sun. 'You take our torc with you an' you'll die. That torc belongs to us, 'tis the O'Brien torc, and there's a death curse on anyone who steals it.'

The bounty hunter laughed. 'We all gotta die, girl,

but I gotta kind a notion you gonna die 'fore I do. Ain't that right, Charlie?' And the two of them wheeled their horses and galloped away through the dust to the head of the column.

Sean and Annie looked on, tears of fury welling up inside them as the wagon-train trundled slowly by, creaking and groaning over the rocky ground. They watched together in silence as the last wagon rolled into the shimmering haze and out of their sight. But as it did so they saw a rider coming back and soon recognised him as Matt Colby. As he rode up, he unslung two water bottles and let them gently down to the ground in front of them. The Colonel looked up at him. 'Thanks, Matt,' he said. 'That was kind of you.'

'Colonel,' said Matt Colby, and there was a catch in his voice. 'You gotta believe I didn't want no part of this. But I was on my own, Colonel, and I had my family to think of. He's the only one knows the way out of this hell, Colonel, and there weren't nothin' I could do to stop him. You've gotta believe I didn't know they was gonna leave you without your mules and without your water. You gotta believe me.'

'I believe you well enough, Matt,' said the Colonel, getting to his feet and taking Matt Colby's outstretched hand. 'We'll be fine, Matt. Now we got your water we'll be fine. Someone will be along the trail before too long. You get along back to your family, they'll be needing you.'

'If you can make 'em see sense, Colonel,' said Matt Colby, 'I'll take Sean and Annie with me. It's their last chance. Ain't nothin' more I can do.'

'We'll not be going with you, Mr Colby,' said Sean in a manner so final that Matt Colby knew that argument would be fruitless.

'We'll make it,' said the Colonel. 'On your way now, Matt.' And Matt Colby rode away from them, stopping only once to look over his shoulder. The Colonel bent down and picked up the water bottles carefully. He shook them gently and smiled. 'Brim full,' he said. 'He's a fine man.'

'How can you be saying that?' said Sean, 'after what he's done?'

'In his place,' said the Colonel, 'I'd have done the same thing. He had his family, children, and he had to protect them as best he could. Man's duty.' And they watched the horse until it vanished into the horizon. Then he turned to the children, smiling ruefully. 'Well, my little soldiers, we'll not be down-hearted, will we? Eh, Annie? Remember California –

if I'm right it's not more than a few weeks over those mountains. I'm not sure you should have stayed with me, children, but I'll be for ever grateful that you did. Means a lot to your old Colonel and he won't forget it. I'm sorry we lost the torc – know how much it means to you both. But you lost it once before remember, and we got it back. We've lost a battle, children, but the war is still to be won. We've the wagon for shelter, and your revolver is in my trunk, Sean. So we can hunt and eat. And thanks to Matt we now have some water at least. It's not much, but it may be enough. There's a full moon so we'll travel only in the cool of the night – save our water that way. We rest up by day and march by night. Soon as the sun goes down this evening I'll try and shoot us some supper – got to be a snake somewhere's about here with nothing better to do than feed us. Meanwhile it's under that wagon with you and we'll lie still so as we don't use up any more of that water than we've got to.'

The wagon was some protection against the cruel sun, but soon enough their throats dried so that it hurt to swallow and they were forced to take tiny sips of water to keep their lips from cracking. They tried to sleep but could not. Each was alone now with his own thoughts and none of them wanted to share the fears that haunted them.

At sundown the Colonel left them with strict instructions to stay by the wagon. They were to break up the empty water barrel on the wagon for firewood and have it burning by the time he got back in an hour or so. They heard some time later a single gunshot and lit the fire in eager anticipation that supper was on its way. But the Colonel's hour went by and another and another and still there was no sign of him. Annie was all for venturing out on to the moonlit desert to find him, but Sean remembered the Colonel's orders and managed to restrain her.

CHAPTER 30

THEY WERE SITTING SIDE BY SIDE, FEET DANGLING over the back of the wagon, and straining to pick up some movement in the desert, when they heard a distant shuffling that turned gradually into the slow uneven tread of a man. 'You got that fire going?' came the Colonel's voice out of the desert. And as he spoke they saw at last the Colonel's tall silhouette limping slowly towards them. 'Got us a fine fat snake, children,' he said as he approached.

'What's the matter, Mister Colonel, what happened to you?' said Annie running up to meet him.

'A little fall,' said the Colonel, limping painfully

towards the fire leaning heavily on Annie's shoulder. 'Couldn't rightly see where I was going and then my blasted leg gave out on me. Took me a while to get back. Be fine when I've rested it up. Won't be able to march on it tonight, I'm afraid. But no matter, with this snake inside us we'll feel stronger and we've still got a whole water bottle left, haven't we, Sean?'

'Yes, Colonel,' said Sean. ''Tis nearly a bottle and a half.' But he caught a glimpse of the Colonel's face by the light of the fire. It was pale and drawn and twisted into a grimace of agony as he sat down to skin the snake. And Sean noticed that the Colonel ate very little of the snake but insisted that they should finish it between them. He felt uneasy but did not know why.

'Will you play something for me, Sean?' said the Colonel, as he sat by the fire after supper was finished. He had lit a cigar and was resting with his back against the wheel of the wagon, his leg stretched out in front of him. 'And you must sing, Annie. It will soothe my leg; and if you play well and sing well I shall treat you to a tot of whiskey to keep out the cold of the night. I know it's against my rules, but this is special. And I want happy tunes, do you hear? None of your Irish melancholy. Do I have a bargain?'

'A bargain,' they said and Sean took out his fiddle and Annie fetched her moon-shawl from the trunk and wrapped it round the Colonel's shoulders before they began. The Colonel clapped his knee as he always did and called for encore after encore as the reels and jigs echoed out across the desert and banished the terrible dread that tugged inside each of them.

The Colonel was true to his word and had Annie delve into the bottom of his trunk for his precious bottle of whiskey that he handed round, leaving himself till last. 'Now to bed, children,' he said, 'for tomorrow we have to make up what we lost today. It's only two nights' march westwards and we'll be out of the desert. We shall do it, children, never fear. I haven't brought you this far to have you die in the desert. Now sleep. We can sleep through 'till the heat of the day is gone and set off at dusk.'

'And what about your leg, Colonel?' Sean asked.

'Oh, it'll be fine in the morning, never you fear,' said the Colonel. 'Now give your old Colonel a kiss and get under those blankets. The nights are cold out here. I shall smoke one more cigar before I join you – maybe two.'

The children said their prayers more fervently

than ever that night, but the whiskey served its purpose and they were asleep before the worries over the perils ahead of them, over their diminishing supply of water, could begin to gnaw at them. They did not wake until they felt the sun beating down through the canvas of the wagon. Sean was the first to notice that the Colonel's blanket lay folded neatly as he always left it. He leapt from the wagon to find the ashes of the fire still warm, and three cigar butts pressed into the sand where the Colonel had been sitting. The snake skin was curled up and dried in the sun. His call brought Annie out of the wagon. They consoled themselves with the possibility that the Colonel had gone off hunting again, until they found Sean's revolver under the Colonel's blanket.

'Mister Colonel!' Annie called out, hands cupped to her mouth. 'Where are you, Mister Colonel?' But the desert lay empty about them and threw back only her words in reply. It was then as a sudden breeze shook the canvas of the wagon that Sean noticed a piece of white paper flapping under the lid of the Colonel's trunk. He had to open it before he could pull the paper free. As he read, his worst fears were confirmed.

My dear children,

I am not a medical man but I fear my leg is finished. It never was very good as you know – blame the Mexicans for that. But a man with only one good leg cannot walk far. I could not keep up with you for one mile. I should slow you both down and would use what little water you have to no avail. So I am leaving you to go on alone. I would not do so were I not sure you will reach California.

Follow the trail of the wagons if you can. It cannot be more than two days' march to the edge of the desert. Beyond that you will find trees and food and water. Take your cloak and your shawl and use them as a tent against the sun. Lie up by day as I told you and walk hard at night. The revolver you will find under my blanket. You will find bullets enough as well.

So I have lost my last battle, children – but then everyone does. But when you reach your valley and find your father, as I know you will, please write to Henry and Martha and tell them I tried to help. Tell them to remember me well if they can and I trust you will too, my dear children. I won't be seeing the Pacific after all – you'll have to see it for me. My last order to you is this. Do not attempt to

find me. It is an old soldier's dying wish that you
should obey that order.
Your Mister Colonel

Annie took the letter from his hand and read it in silence. They clung to each other then and wept for the friend they had lost; but it was Annie who broke away first, brushing the tears from her cheeks. 'We'll not be giving up, Sean,' she said. 'Not after what Mister Colonel has done for us.' But Sean could not raise his crumpled spirits to meet hers. She shook him by the shoulders. 'We have to try, Sean,' she said. 'For the Colonel's sake. He's left us all the water has he not? We have to try.'

It took all that day for Annie to persuade her brother that all hope had not vanished with the Colonel. They lay side by side under the shade of the wagon, and slowly her words began to tell on him, to break through the cloud of grief that over-shadowed him. She spoke of the torc that was but a day or so ahead of them and still recoverable, of their father waiting for them in California that was only weeks away now over the mountains. She spoke of Will, of Fiddler Donnelly, of Little Luke and Bessie, of Henry and Martha, and how they had all helped them on their way. 'And are we to give up now? Are we, Sean?'

Sean said little or nothing, but lay listening to her until the sun began to lose its heat. Quite suddenly he took her by the hand and they crawled out together from under the wagon. He looked down into his sister's face and she could see the life back in his eyes. 'He was the best man I ever knew, Annie,' he said, 'and I shall be as near like him as I can when I'm grown. Well, what are you waiting for, Annie? We'd better be going. 'Tis like the Colonel said, we've a hell of a way to go.'

The trail of wagons was not difficult to follow for even where the sand had covered the wheelruts there was always the discarded flotsam of the wagon-train to follow, frequent horse droppings, abandoned belongings and once the stiff carcase of a used-up mule. They took with them only the fiddle case, with the Colonel's last letter pushed inside, the remaining water bottle that was still full and Miss Henry's revolver. Sean wore Will's cloak around his shoulders to keep out the chill of the night and Annie walked beside him wrapped in her moon-shawl that gleamed white in the moonlight. They spoke hardly a word but concentrated on the trail ahead, keeping an eye always on the horizon for the first glimmer of dawn in the east that would force them to look for shelter. And when it came at last they were glad of it for their feet throbbed with pain and all the strength was drained from their legs.

As the sun came up they stretched the cloak and the moon-shawl out over two standing rocks, weighted them down with boulders, and lay down to sleep through the heat of the day. They treated themselves to a mouthful of water each and kept it long in the mouth, swirling it around and savouring it before they swallowed it.

Annie lay looking up at the pattern of her shawl against the early sun when Sean tapped her shoulder. He was sitting up and pointing into the grey desert dawn. There in the far distance the horizon turned suddenly black and green as it rose to mountains beyond. 'The Colonel was right,' he said. 'One more day and we'll be into those trees, and where there's trees there'll be water, Annie.' And they both curled up beside the fiddle case, new-found hope obliterating their unsatisfied thirst, their empty, aching stomachs.

But the next night the kind moon had left them and the desert was black about them. They soon lost the trail of the wagons they had followed so well, and knowing their water bottle was now less than half-full they increased their pace.

The march began well, a downhill trek across the desert that seemed to be sinking before them into a flat basin, but although Sean insisted they were going westward towards the invisible trees, he felt less than sure of himself as the hours passed. As dawn came up they found themselves in an empty expanse of arid desert. They could find nothing on which they could rig up their shelter. There were no rocks, no cacti, nothing but flat, heat-cracked desert stretching ahead of them into nowhere. When the sun fell on the line of green in the distance and lit up the mountains beyond, they seemed scarcely closer than the day before. No discussion was needed, both knew that they had no alternative but to walk on through the dreadful heat that beat down on them and turned their legs weak at the knees and sent their heads spinning. They covered their heads against the sun and stumbled and staggered over ever rockier ground that began now to rise ahead of them so that each step became a huge effort of will. Only the shimmering, beckoning green through the haze kept their legs going, but Sean felt Annie slowing all the time and knew she had not much more to give. The time had come, he thought, for them to finish the last of the water. Once they started drinking, neither had the will to resist drinking all they could. Renewed and revitalised, Sean helped her to her feet again. They linked arms and went on.

However high they climbed, the trees ahead seemed higher and the mountains beyond came no closer. Every few steps now they paused to regain their breath, to will away the whirling inside their heads and the blurring of the world around them. At last Annie's legs would no longer do her bidding and she sank to her knees among the rocks and tried to crawl. Sean had not the strength to lift her and none of his exhortations could persuade her back to her feet. She simply shook her head and cried. When her arms could no longer hold her weight she lay down amongst the rocks to die. Sean lay down beside her and covered her with her moon-shawl.

''Tis a pity we lost the torc, Sean,' she whispered. ''Tis a terrible pity.'

CHAPTER 31

FROM HIGH UP IN THE TREES, SEAMUS FINN combed the desert below him with his telescope. The Blackrock Desert was a place to be avoided – he knew that well enough for he had crossed it all those years before when he first came out west. 'A graveyard of a place,' he muttered to himself and snapped the telescope shut. 'Sure there's not a bear fool enough to set foot out there, and certainly not this bear.' And he raised his voice calling into the trees around him. 'You've cost me a week of me life you divil,' he shouted. 'I been trackin' you for a week now. An' if you're peekin' out from behind one of those trees, an' I'm thinkin' you will be, then don't think you've seen the last of me, mister bear. Maybe you've got away this time, but there's always a next time. I'm goin' back home, mister bear. Tell you what, I'll make a bargain with you: you leave my traps well alone and I'll leave you alone. Is it a bargain we have?'

The old mountain man was just turning away when out of the corner of his eye he saw something white fluttering at the edge of the desert below him. His telescope focussed on the spot and picked out the figure of a boy standing on a boulder and waving a white cloth over his head. He could see he was shouting, but no sound carried up into the trees. 'Jasus, Mary Mother of God,' he said crossing himself. 'Will you look what it is out there? Will you just look. And now I suppose you'll be wantin' me to bring him back, won't you? An' what the divil's a young boy like that doing out there and all on his own? And don't I have enough troubles without addin' to them? All spring an' summer out here an' not a sign of the gold you promised me an' a terrible inconvenient bear that springs every trap I put down. All right, Mary, all right, I'm goin', but 'tis under sufferance, under sufferance. 'Tis not fair on a man, not fair at all.'

Sean went on shouting and waving until he was

sure it was indeed a horse and rider moving down through the trees towards him. The man's distant bellowing had come to him as he lay by Annie's side. He had thought himself crazed by the heat and dust and refused to believe the evidence of his ears. And when he first saw what appeared to be a horse's head tossing in the trees, he was almost sure it was an hallucination. He knew of the tricks a mirage could play on the eyes, but the horse kept coming on and so he kept shouting until his voice was sore with it and until there was no doubt that his senses were not deceiving him.

'An' where the divil did you come from, young man?' said Seamus Finn looking down at Sean from his horse. 'An' who is that you have with you?'

''Tis my sister, Annie, and she's near dying, mister, for want of water,' said Sean. 'Would you have some water, mister?'

'To be sure I have, young man,' said Seamus Finn handing down his canteen and dismounting. Sean bent over his sister and lifted her head from the sand and poured the water in between her burnt lips. She struggled at first until Seamus Finn held her arms still and then she coughed herself back to life as the water trickled down her throat.

'Thank you mister,' said Sean. 'So we're not lost after all.' And then under his breath. 'You were right, Colonel. You always were.'

'Sure I'm no colonel,' said Seamus Finn. 'An' I should say you were about as lost as a young man can be.' The old mountain man's great white eyebrows twitched under his hat. 'By the talk of you, you could be an Irishman,' he went on. 'No, but 'tis not possible, too much to hope for. You wouldn't be an Irishman, I suppose? 'Tis years since I heard those dulcet tones from a man. 'Bout here they grunt and spit more'n they talk, and do you know there's no one speaks English as sweet as an Irishman. But that's an Irish smile you're wearin', I know it. You're never Irish, young man, are you? You are!'

'County Cork,' said Sean smiling at the old mountain man who knelt by him. He was shorter by a head than Sean himself and possessed a face that glowed like beaten copper in the sun and a fine white head of hair that covered completely his ears and neck. His tiny black-toothed mouth was shrouded in a wispy white moustache that joined a great bush of a beard that was still streaked with gold.

'Kerry, I'm Seamus Finn from Kerry,' said the

mouth, gaping with laughter. 'Jasus, Mary Mother of God, it can't be true. Out here in the middle of nothin' and I run into a lad from County Cork. An' would she be from County Cork too?'

'Course I am,' whispered Annie who had been studying the mountain man's face. 'I'm his sister am I not?'

'Sure you are, darlin',' said Seamus Finn beaming at her. 'An' welcome back to the land of the livin'. Now when your brother's finished my water, an' he looks as if he's every intention of doin' that, then I'll set you both up on old Nod here an' we'll be gettin' out of this terrible place. You'll be on your own I suppose?' Sean and Annie looked back into the desert and said nothing. 'I suppose so then,' said Seamus Finn. 'An' can you walk as far as old Nod, darlin', or shall I be carryin' you?' Sean passed the water canteen back to Annie who gulped it feverishly. 'Slowly, darlin', slowly. Take all you like, but slowly – you don't want to flood yourself inside – an' there'll be plenty more where that came from, plenty more.'

They made camp that evening in a different world. A tumbling stream washed down from the mountain above them and Seamus Finn turned a haunch of venison on a spit over the fire so that the smell of it pervaded the air around them. He talked incessantly, so glad was he of the company. He could not get over the good fortune of coming across his fellow countrymen and would punctuate his monologue with repeated thanks to the Blessed Mary. But the children were strangely sad and quiet he thought, and try as he did he could not drag a smile from them as they sat together by the fire.

'And to think,' he went on. 'And to think I didn't really want to fetch you in. I didn't, honest. If the Blessed Mary hadn't kicked me up the backside, you'd be lying out there now, I'm sure of it. Maybe it was meant somehow. I've been talkin' to nothin' but the birds and beasts and a few Indians for near enough ten years or more. I've had a word or two with the Blessed Mary, but she's often too busy elsewhere to listen for long. Anyways, I'm a terrible wicked man and she wouldn't want to be passing the time of day with the likes of me, not unless she's got to. Been trappin' up here all that time. Met a Russian or two, a few Frenchmen and I've known the odd American – you see 'em all down at Sutter's Fort where I take my skins for trading – but in all that time I've never met another proper Irishman. Jasus, Mary Mother of God, I think I could die of happiness. Course I'd be happier still with a pile of gold to go home with. The fur trade's all but finished, you know. They'll still buy the beaver and the fox, an' I can still trap 'em, but 'tis no longer what it was in the old days. Sure the creatures are scarcer now and more wiley. No, 'tis gold I've been after these last two summers. An' all I find is a lot of old rubbish – fools' gold by the bucketful – an' you of course, me darlins, I'm not forgetting you; but I wasn't looking for you, was I now?' And he looked through the smoke of the fire at the two children who sat side by side with their knees drawn up under their chins. There was utter dejection in those eyes that stared into the fire and Seamus Finn was not a man to like gloom or despondency around him, for he knew how it could pull a man down, and he determined to break them free of it. 'I suppose it would be too much to hope that one of you darlins plays that fiddle?' he said.

'Sean plays it,' said Annie.

'Can I look inside, my darlins?' the mountain man asked, reaching for the fiddle case, and Annie nodded. 'What a fine instrument, a fine sight indeed. An' would you want to play it for me, young man? 'Tis a sound I've not heard since I left Ireland. An' 'twould stop old Seamus Finn prattling on, would it not?'

Sean looked across at the old mountain man and shook his head. 'Mr Finn,' he said. 'My heart would not be in it. Fiddler Donnelly – him that taught me how to play it – he said you should never play the fiddle if your heart isn't in it. Told me it was blasphemy to do it. And I'm thinking I won't ever have the heart for it again, not after what happened to the Colonel.'

Annie it was who told the whole story from beginning to end, and Seamus Finn listened, his eyes wide, not in disbelief but in wonder. And when it was over he leaped to his feet, took Annie by her hands and danced a jig around the fire before coming to rest in front of Sean. 'Can you not see, darlins, that 'tis nothin' short of a miracle, all of it? Sure the torc you speak of must be the golden halo of the Blessed Mary herself. Nothin' else could work such a miracle. An' didn't it get you here, her halo? An' why would you be needin' it any more when I'm here now an' 'tis no more'n a month over the mountains down to Grass Valley? I've been through it myself on the way up here. 'Tis no distance. You'll not be needin' the torc any longer. So you've nothin' at all to be sad about, young man, nothin' at all. An' tell me somethin', would that Fiddler of yours want you to stop your playin', or Little Luke, or your Colonel? Answer me that, young man. Sure 'tis they who kept you alive in this beautiful world. Your Colonel gave his life for it and will you repay him now by grievin'? Do you not remember, young man, that when someone dies back in Ireland after a fine life, do we not hold a wake? Do we not dance and sing? Do we mope? Do we weep? Never. So now, right now, we'll hold a wake and we'll dance and sing for your Colonel. Take the fiddle Sean O'Brien, and make the music. It'll keep your souls nearer to God and to the Blessed Mary herself. Sure they'll all be lookin' down on us from up there and joinin' in. After all, 'tis not unheard of for the Angels to sing if they've a mind to, is it now?'

And so Sean played his fiddle again and Seamus Finn and Annie sang together the old songs and he danced a jig or two as well as he could, but his old legs would not move as they should so that at the last he tripped himself up and fell in an ungainly heap by the fire. And as he sat up he saw that the two children were laughing with him and he marvelled at them.

That night as he curled his body into a tight

warming ball, his hands pushed between his knees as they always were, the old mountain man whispered to himself, 'Jasus, Mary Mother of God, will you look at those two darlins. Would you just look at them?'

'Mr Finn,' said Annie from the other side of the fire. 'Will you take us down to Grass Valley to see our father?'

'No bother, darlins,' said Seamus Finn. 'No bother at all. There's still a month or so of autumn left, an' that's good pannin' time, but I don't suppose another four weeks lookin' for gold will do me an awful lot of good. I tell you what, darlins, we'll pass by my cabin and collect the few skins that infernal bear left me before we go down to find your father. Sure there's enough there to keep me in drink through the winter months, an' that's all that matters to an old man. And if the gold is there, it'll be there next year, won't it now?'

CHAPTER 32

OLD NOD WAS THE SLOWEST-MOVING HORSE Annie had ever seen, but her pace was constant uphill, downhill, with Annie riding on her or with all three of them up, she plodded on, head hanging low and sighing deeply from time to time. 'Sure she should never have been a horse,' said Seamus Finn. 'I've had her all her life and she's never liked being a horse. Told me time and again, she has.'

'Does she speak to you often?' Annie asked, leaning over to pat old Nod's scrawny neck.

'Constantly,' said Seamus Finn, 'she's no one else to talk to, has she now? An' she's wonderful company too. Whatever I tell her she agrees with.

Look at her nodding away there. Now could a man ever have a wife who did that? I think not. Anyway, I'll not be gettin' a better-lookin' wife at my age, will I now? An' she certainly won't be gettin' a better lookin' husband – that's for sure.'

All the way back over the sierras that rose and plunged ahead of them, Seamus Finn paused to check his traps so that by the time they reached the cabin a week later a cluster of pelts hung down over the side of Nod's withers. The cabin was a squat, untidy construction of logs with a single door and window and a chimney. At one end it was piled to the ceiling with furs. Inside and out it reminded the children of home. And old Seamus Finn made them feel at home. They would stop there only long enough to stretch the skins dry in the sun, just a few days at the most, Seamus Finn said, and then they'd be off down the mountains to find their father. But while they were waiting they might just as well pass the time in panning the river that rushed by not a hundred yards below the cabin – just in case.

'Sure there's nothin' to it, darlins,' he said the first evening over supper, 'you just shovel the pay dirt from the river bank into me frying-pan here, take out the few sticks, add a touch of water and swirl it round so that she soil is taken off by the water. The gold when you find it will lie heavy and stay in the bottom of the pan – you'll notice it for sure for 'tis yellow as the sun and will glow at you. Sure, 'tis simplicity itself. Nothin' to it, nothin' at all.'

'Then why is it you haven't found any, Seamus Finn?' Annie asked. 'Seeing it's that simple.'

'Darlin', you've a cruel tongue for such a pretty girl,' said Seamus Finn. 'Has she not, young man? Does she not cut you to the quick? There's hundreds of folk diggin' away down-river, but they don't know what I know. No one does. 'Tis me secret, me darlins, but I'll share it with you because I've been longin' to share it with someone I can trust, an' there's not many of them about. Two years ago it was, an old Indian chief came by while I was camping by the river down there an' he told me I would find gold, so much gold I'd be the richest man in all the world. The old divil, he told me there was so much of it the water ran yellow from the mountain. A man believes what he wants to believe, me darlins. So I built me cabin and for two hot summers long I've dug an' I've panned. 'Tis here, darlins, I know 'tis here. I feel it in me nose, but I've not been able to find it, not yet. Now, with two extra pairs of fresh young eyes on the job we could snap up a fortune, darlins, a mighty fortune and I could be off back home to Ireland where I belong. But I'll not go back a poor man. I told 'em all when I left I'd be back with enough money to buy half of Kerry or I'd not come back at all.'

Sean and Annie had little choice but to agree, for each had a frying-pan thrust into their hands and they followed him obediently down to the river's edge where the old mountain man demonstrated the art of gold panning with consummate skill and a dramatic commentary. They were reluctant at first for the water was icy cold, and anyway they longed only to get down out of the mountain into Grass Valley where their father would be waiting for them, but as they panned that first evening the gold fever took them and they had almost to be dragged back to the cabin when night fell.

The days passed into weeks and old Seamus Finn, on his knees in the water beside them, seemed less and less inclined to leave for Grass Valley. The skins, he always said, needed just a few days more drying time. Lack of success began now to dampen the children's earlier ardour and they moved away from Seamus Finn as often as they could up-stream and out of sight. And here in the heat of the day they would cavort and splash in the stream and then lie out in the warmth of the sun to dry off and listen to Seamus Finn's croaky renderings of 'The Munster Lass', or 'The Little Yellow Boy'.

On just such a morning in late October Sean was lying flat out on a rock over the river and reaching in under its shade to tickle a trout, whilst Annie lay dreaming on the bank beside him. Downstream they could hear Seamus Finn hurling abuse at the dirt in the bottom of his pan, when Annie sat up suddenly. 'Listen,' she said.

''Tis only Seamus cursing again, Annie,' said Sean.

'Not that. Listen,' she whispered. Sean lifted his hand out of the water and heard the voices at once and the sound of hooves among the trees up-stream. The Indians came down from the woods towards them, a party of a dozen or more, bare-back on solid little ponies that picked their feet up delicately as they splashed across the stream.

Sean and Annie moved like gazelles as they leapt from rock to rock along the bank of the river. A look over their shoulders told them that the Indians were gaining on them and they knew they had to warn Seamus Finn before it was too late. They had to take the shortest way back across the river to where Seamus Finn was kneeling over his pan. They floundered into the deep water shouting to him, but the ice-cold water took the breath from their bodies and no words came out, only cries. Seamus Finn ignored them; he knew the children would be playing as they always did. He was swirling the water around in his pan, screwing his eyes tight, trying to focus on the residue left behind. Only when the children had finally crossed the river and were running towards him and screaming did he look up, and that was only because yet again he was left with a pan of colourless, murky silt.

'An' what are you two hollerin' about, you little divils?' he shouted. And he followed their pointing arms to the band of Indians that was galloping down on him.

CHAPTER 33

'WILL YOU STOP YOUR NONSENSE?' SAID SEAMUS
Finn, throwing away his frying-pan. 'Will you stop
your hollerin', you'll frighten them away. They'll not
be hurtin' you. They're just Indians, friends of mine
you might say. An' he's the old chief I was tellin' you
about, darlins, the one who told me the river was
yellow with gold. An' every time he's set eyes on me
since, he laughs till he cries, the old divil. He's
laughin' now, just look at him, the old divil.'

And sure enough the old Indian was bent over his
horse, consumed with laughter. They were a party of
young braves with hard, dark bodies and steely eyes.
There was a severity about them that alarmed the two

children as they sheltered behind Seamus Finn. Each of the braves carried a rifle except for the old chief who went unarmed. But Seamus Finn left the children and advanced towards the Indians, his hand held high in the air. 'Will you just stay where you are, me darlins,' he said as he walked away, 'an' there'll be no trouble, no trouble at all. If there's one thing I've learnt about an Indian it's that he needs to know whether you're a friend or an enemy. There's nothing much in between, not for him and not for me, come to that. An' just now I think I'd prefer to be his friend, wouldn't you? So not a word, me darlins, not a word.' And he began to talk animatedly to the elderly chief who laughed incessantly as he spoke. The old mountain man spoke a language the children could not understand. They listened, trying to make some sense out of what was being said, but they could not, for they spoke in a strange language of long resonant vowels and dramatic gestures, all of which were quite incomprehensible to them.

Annie was patient for a while, as patient as she could be, but she was not one to be left out of any conversation for very long. 'What's he talking about?' she called out after a while. 'What do they want?'

'He's gettin' round to it,' said Seamus Finn in a

language they could understand again, but he did not turn round as he spoke. 'The old divil's hinting he has something he'd like to sell us – something he thinks I would like to buy.' And the Indian chief spoke again, expansively and at great length. The laughter had stopped now and some anger crept into his tone in the middle of the story before the laughter resumed.

When he had finished, Seamus Finn interpreted quietly for the children. 'He says his village was attacked, maybe a week back, by two migrants from a wagon-train. Says they came to buy his horses but he refused. Says in the battle that followed he lost three of his young braves, five squaws and a girl child of six years old. Says he hunted them down and killed both of them. Don't be gettin' excited now, me darlins, but the old divil says they found around the neck of one of them what he calls a "twist of gold". Now I know what you'll be thinkin', me darlins, an' I'm thinkin' much the same sort of thing, but you're to keep your face as flat as a pancake, not so much as a glitter in your eye, do you hear now? The old divil's wonderin' whether I'd be interested in buying such a thing. He's no use for gold himself, he says. I think he's thumbin' his nose at me 'cos he's found gold and I haven't. Now for pity's sake, darlins, you're not to say a thing while I negotiate with the old divil. If you look even a little interested he'll have the skin off my back.'

Sean and Annie swallowed back the joy that threatened to burst from them. Neither of them had forgotten the loss of the torc, but they had quite given up any hope of recovering it. They had simply come to terms with the finality of its loss. Annie's hand slipped into Sean's and squeezed it white. She clenched her jaw muscles tight to stop her lips from trembling, and did her very best to look nonchalant. Seamus Finn shrugged his shoulders and looked mildly interested as one of the young braves rode up alongside his chief and handed over the golden torc. The chief passed it down to Seamus Finn who examined it almost casually, and then, to the dismay of the children, handed it back and shook his head dismissively. Annie could stand it no longer. 'Buy it, Mr Finn,' she cried out, running up to him. ''Tis our torc, you know it is. You must buy it, Mr Finn. You can't let it go, not now. We'll pay you back, Mr Finn, honest we will, soon as we get to Grass Valley Father will pay you back.'

The old mountain man's shoulders slumped and he shook his head. 'Oh Annie, darlin', do you imagine I didn't know it was your torc an' that you'd not like it back? Did you imagine that? There couldn't be two such wonderful objects out in these mountains, could there now? I was just about to persuade the old divil it was worth a few good pelts, an' I think he would have been quite happy with that. The last thing I wanted was for him to know how important it was to us. An' now, by the look on his face, I'm thinkin' that maybe he knows we'd pay him the earth for it. Annie, darlin', you're the sweetest thing on earth, but when it comes to matters of business you've got the brain of a donkey, have you not? Old Seamus was doin' fine for you, would have got your torc back for next to nothing. Look at the old divil now, Annie, just look at the glint in his eye. He's no fool, Annie darlin'. He knows now I'll give him every pelt I have to possess his twist of gold. An' I will, Annie, darlin', I will.'

And so he did. Not only the skins piled up in the cabin, but even those stretched out in the sun were cut down and handed over. Every one of the horses was loaded with pelts until the cabin was quite empty. All the while the old chief laughed and Seamus Finn put a brave face on it and laughed back. He watched them ride away up the river, taking with them his year's work, and then he turned to Annie, the torc in his hand. He smiled at her and stroked her long hair. Then he opened the torc and fastened it around her neck. 'You'll be the ruin of me, darlin',' he said, and he kissed her gently on the cheek before turning away and walking slowly uphill towards the cabin. They could see he was trying to make light of it, and Annie wanted to catch him by the hand and tell him she was sorry, but she could not bring herself to do it. ''Tis about time we left the mountains, darlins,' he said as he reached the cabin. 'We'll be leavin' first light tomorrow, so I'll be off to find us some supper now. Mind you keep close to the cabin, me darlins.'

Sean and Annie sat silent on the sandy beach by the river, Annie full of deep remorse for what she had done and Sean trying to refrain from speaking of it. What was done, he thought, was done, and there was little point in rubbing salt into the wound. Neither could feel any joy that the torc was theirs again, at the way good fortune had smiled on them. They could think only of the weariness they had seen in Seamus Finn's old face as the Indians had ridden off with his beloved skins slung across their horses. Angry, Sean picked up the discarded frying-pan with both hands and stabbed the handle into the sand beside him. It did not sink in deep as he had expected but struck something hard that jarred his wrist. He dug his hand deep into the sand and scooped it away until the jagged stone he had struck was laid bare to the sun. Sean thought it strange at first that the stone should catch and hold the yellow of the sun for they were high up on the beach and the sand about him was dull and dry as a bone. He was on his hands and knees now digging feverishly to prise the stone clear. Annie was alone with her thoughts, throwing pebbles into the river one after the other and muttering under her breath. She paid him no attention at first.

'Annie,' he called, suppressing the gleam in his voice, 'could I be looking at the torc please? Would you let me have it for a moment?'

Annie unclasped it and handed it over. 'I don't want it anyway,' she said. 'I don't care if I never see it again. It's killed one good man and ruined another. It has a curse on it, Sean, I know it has.' Sean ignored her, and with the torc in his hands walked on his knees back to the stone. Then he laid it in the sand beside the stone to be quite sure he was sure, and only then did he call Annie over.

CHAPTER 34

SEAMUS FINN CAME BACK EMPTY-HANDED AN hour later. He was surprised to find the children waiting for him in the cabin, sitting quietly at the table, an upturned frying-pan between them. The hour spent hunting had been enough for him to reason away the disaster that had befallen him. It had happened, he decided, in retribution of his wicked past. Up in the woods he had spoken philosophically to the Blessed Mary. 'Do I have a clean sheet now?' he had asked. 'Is that all you're going to do to me, Mother Mary?' And by the time he reached the cabin he had convinced himself it was.

The children seemed sombre as they sat, eyes

lowered to the table, and he knew them well enough to expect them to be like that. 'Not me day, darlins,' he said cheerfully, leaning his rifle up by the door. 'Shot an' missed five times, not a thing I'm proud of, not at all. Maybe I'm gettin' old at last. Only look in the mirror once a year, me darlins, a man keeps younger that way, or maybe he just thinks he does. But no matter, we can take a fish or two out of the river at dusk, can we not, Sean?' And still the children sat silent and unmoved. 'Now you'll not be carryin' on like that all evenin', will you darlins, will you now? 'Twas not that bad. Let's just call it a little disaster. I've had a few of them in my time an' you've had a few in yours. Somethin' will turn up for Seamus Finn me darlins, always has done, always will do. So stop your mopin'. 'Twasn't your fault, Annie darlin', 'twas no one's fault, an' there's an end of it.'

'I've got something for you, Mr Finn,' said Annie quietly. 'Maybe it'll make up for the pelts I lost you.'

'You're a sweet child, Annie O'Brien,' said the old mountain man, 'but I'll not hear of it darlin', I'll not hear of it.'

''Tis under the frying-pan on the table, Mr Finn,' said Annie. 'Will you not take a look?'

'I think maybe you should,' said Sean. 'Sure she's been to an awful lot of trouble for you Mr Finn.'

As he lifted the frying-pan Seamus Finn's heart stopped beating inside him. The nugget of gold lay on the table in the light of the open door. It was the size of his fist, shaped like a little jagged boot. He picked it up carefully and nestled it in his hands as one might a chicken's egg. His heart started again and pumped so wildly that his head swam and he had to steady himself against the table. There was the glitter of gold right through the stone. He ran out of the door into the sunlight to look at it more closely. He tried first one eye, then the other, for he trusted neither. Then he bit it at its pointed end and lifted it up like an offering to heaven. 'Holy Mary, Mother of God,' he said, and he fell on his knees in the dust. 'Oh you darlins, you little darlins! I've seen enough fools' gold to know this is the real thing. Oh you darlins!' And he stood up as the children ran out of the cabin and into his arms, and they knelt beside him and prayed with him as the old mountain man thanked the Blessed Mary.

That night the fiddle played as never before and the old mountain man danced Annie to a standstill. All that stopped it was the bow on the fiddle that finally lost its last few hairs. Seamus Finn tried to mend it with a string, but it was not the same after that, and the torc went back inside the fiddle where it belonged and the case was closed.

They stayed up in the hills for another week or more. At the end of that time they had found as much gold as old Nod could carry down the mountain. Chipping and panning and digging, they followed the streak of gold along the river bank until it ran out. 'There's enough in there,' said Seamus Finn, patting the saddle bags, 'to buy all of Ireland. But I'm not a greedy man an' I don't want all of it. I'll settle for just a large chunk of Kerry. An' that's where I'll go, darlins, I'll go back to Kerry like I said an' buy the lot of it. 'Tis me dream, little darlins, me dream come true. I came to this country to make me fortune, but I'm Irish born an' I'll be going back there to die; an' now I'll die on me own land, in me own house, an' that's an awful good feelin' for an old man to have.'

Old Nod stumbled under the weight of the gold. Most of the going was downhill along the Feather River. They were careful to look miserable as they passed the prospectors that crawled like ants all over the valleys. They shook their heads sadly when asked if they had had any luck, and Annie made a point of looking even more wretched than any of them, but Seamus Finn never quite trusted her tongue and kept her by his side whenever they met company to be sure the tongue did not wag once again. They took turns to ride up on old Nod and progress was slow. But within three weeks they rode down into Grass Valley.

It was balmy and green as Annie had dreamed in her dreams but the hills were browner and more rolling, and the pine trees were not so tall, but there was a silver glinting river running through the valley and this they followed. All the while now they were looking for their father and asking after him. Every tall man they saw made their hearts jump in anticipation, but they were always disappointed. And every shake of the head sent their hopes plummeting.

At every shack now they stopped to ask for Patrick O'Brien, but no one seemed to know him. They stopped riders as they passed by and described the tall, ginger-haired Irishman, but no one knew of him. Every time they spied a house with a tall chimney their spirits rose, only to be dashed again. It was only the old mountain man's cheerful faith that kept any spark of hope alive in the children that they would find their father. He would not let them sink into a gloomy silence, nor dwell on the awful possibility that grew more and more real every day that their father had never reached this valley, that they would never find him alive. It was during these anxious days that the two children came to love the old mountain man deeply, and for his part Seamus Finn never ceased to wonder at these two children who had come through so much.

They came one noontime to a cluster of shacks by the riverside where two children played barefoot in the grass chasing chickens, sending them running on tiptoe, wings outstretched and squawking in under the sanctuary of a delapidated wagon. Annie was about to protest to them when an angry mother threw open the door of the shack and screamed at her children to stop persecuting the creatures or they would be early to bed that night. Seamus Finn called out to her from the track. 'Beggin' your pardon, Ma'am, but we're lookin' for the house of one Patrick O'Brien, lately come from County Cork in Ireland. Do you know the man I'm speaking of by any chance?'

'Sure I do, sir,' said the mother, coming out on to her verandah and wiping her hands on her apron. 'His place is half a day's ride down along the valley.

It's the only house you'll find. Built himself a fine place he has, tallest chimney I ever did see. But no one's seen him for a couple of months now, not since he came back. Are you kin of his maybe?'

'We are,' said Annie, putting her arms around her brother's neck and squeezing him tight. 'Are we not, Sean?'

'Son and daughter,' said Sean. 'I'm the son and she's the daughter.'

'I can tell that much,' said the mother, laughing in the sun as she pushed back her hair from her forehead. 'Just about given you up he has, I reckon. Seems you took a long time acoming. That's going to be a mighty happy house tonight, mighty happy. Keep along the river this side of the bank, and you can't miss it. Don't take the track going south, just keep along the river and you'll find it.'

'Ma'am,' said Seamus Finn, 'I'll be needin' another horse an' saddle. I see you've some fine animals in the paddock. I'd pay you well, Ma'am, in gold, in proper gold.'

'Gold? You mean real, live gold?'

'Yes Ma'am,' said Seamus Finn. 'Old Nod here has just about worn herself out an' I'll be needin' a mount to take me so far as San Francisco. That roan over there, she'd do me fine, Ma'am.'

The deal was made and the delighted lady ushered her bedraggled dusty children into the house still gazing in disbelief at the lump of gold in her hand.

Annie led the way now, urging on old Nod who condescended at times to break into a laboured trot, but it would only be a few paces before she had returned to her habitual plod. No amount of shouting and kicking could spur her on. 'Don't push her, Annie darlin', she'll get you there in her own sweet time, an' that'll be soon enough now.' Seamus Finn fell silent after this. Behind him Sean clung on tight as the skippy roan negotiated the river bank. The two of them were quite happy to listen to Annie as she rambled on about what she would do when she saw her father. 'He'll tell me I've grown,' she said. 'That's what they always say, but it'll be true. He'll pick me up and throw me into the air like he used to, catch me under the arms and swing me high again. And I'll tell him all about how we came here, how the torc brought us back.'

'I'm thinkin' the Blessed Mary had plenty to do with it as well,' said Seamus Finn, at last interrupting her. 'I wouldn't want you to forget that, me darlins, not as long as you live. If there's power in that torc, and I believe there is, then 'tis the Blessed Virgin herself who put it there.'

'And I'll tell him what you did for us, Mr Finn, and he'll ask you to stay, I know he will. He's a fine man, my father,' said Annie, 'a fine man and you'll like him, Mr Finn. I know you'll like him.'

The old mountain man reined up the roan and called on Annie to stop. They let the horses quench their thirst in the river and sat on the bank watching them. Annie was impatient to be on her way, but Seamus Finn laid his hand on her arm. 'Patience, Annie me darlin', patience. By the time you're my age you'll have learnt to be more patient. But you'll not have to be patient for much longer, me darlins, not unless me eyes deceive me. As we came round the bend behind us I saw the top of a chimney in the distance. It'll be your father's house like the lady said. Now I'll not be delayin' you much longer, me darlins, but we've come to the parting of the ways. Your way lies ahead and my way lies south and west to San Francisco, where I'll catch me a boat that will take me back to Kerry where I belong.'

Seamus Finn got to his feet and walked towards the horses, followed by the two children who begged and pleaded with him to stay, but the old mountain man was adamant. He turned to face them and put his arm around each of them. 'I've made me mind up, darlins,' he said. 'You'll not be needin' me any more now, will you? So I'll be going on my way, but before I go, there's somethin' I'd like to give you. We have two saddle bags full of gold and you're to take one of them back to your father. There'll be land to buy and beasts to buy and you can buy all the land in the valley and a mountain or two afterwards as well with what's in this saddle bag. As for myself, I'll be happy with half of Kerry. So take this bag me darlins, an' take old Nod and look after her for me will you?'

But Sean shook his head. ''Tis your gold, Mr Finn, every bit of it. Didn't you come to America to make your fortune? And didn't we come to find our father? And haven't we all found what we came to find? Keep it, Mr Finn.'

But Seamus Finn caught the flicker of disappointment in Annie's eye. 'And cannot an old man leave a parting gift to the prettiest girl in the entire world?' he said, and reached inside the saddle bag and pulled out a nugget of gold the size of a thimble that he pressed into Annie's hand. 'A keepsake, me darlin',' he said. 'Now be on your way before you unman me.'

He helped them up on to old Nod and handed up the black fiddle case to Sean. 'Look after old Nod for me, won't you? And you'll talk to her sometimes for me, me darlins, an' you'll promise me you'll say your prayers to the Blessed Mary every night of your life?'

'We will,' said Annie, sitting up behind Sean on old Nod who chomped noisily at the grass and would not even lift her head to say goodbye to her old master.

'An' if you ever go home to Ireland, you'll come visit me in Kerry. They'll all know me. Just ask for old Seamus Finn, Lord of all Kerry. But don't leave it too long, me darlins, will you now? Old men grow no younger.' And he slapped old Nod on the behind and told her to move on. As the horse moved slowly away the old mountain man shouted after them. 'An' you'll play a tune for me on that fiddle of yours, Sean, from time to time, an' you'll dance for me Annie darlin'? Will you do that now?' Sean dug his heels into old Nod's side and they rode away from him. Strangely, the horse spurred itself for the first time into a canter and the old man's words were drowned by the drumming of the hooves beneath them.

'Let's go home,' said Annie hugging her brother

tight; and later, when the pang of the parting was over, 'Do you think Father'll recognise us, Sean? 'Tis three years since he's seen us. S'pose he doesn't recognise us?'

'We'll know him, won't we?' said Sean, sweetening old Nod on.

'Maybe I'll put on the twist of gold,' she said. 'He'll know it's us then for sure.' And so she did.

It was later that afternoon before they first saw the roof of the house that belonged to the chimney. There were great horned cattle grazing idly down by the river, their tails swishing away the flies. As they rode past, some of them glanced up and lowed at them. The house that came into view slowly was a long, low house with the chimney standing proud at one end and a verandah all around. The windows were orange with the setting sun and the door at the top of the steps was shut fast. There was no sign of life. They dismounted by the rail fence that ran around the house, pushed open the creaky gate and made their way up towards the front door. But before he had gone a few steps, Sean heard a cry behind him and turned to see Annie on her knees beside a newly dug grave. A crude wooden cross stood crooked in the ground.

CHAPTER 35

SEAN AND ANNIE KNELT BY THE GRAVESIDE together. They could not grieve and they could not pray. Despair had drained them of all feeling.

'And what might you be wanting?' came a man's voice. It was a deep resonant voice that both children recognised instantly, and at first they imagined it spoke to them from the grave. 'You're welcome to rest up here for a while.' And when they did not reply: 'Where would you be heading for? 'Tis more than half a day's ride into town.'

Sean and Annie turned to see a tall figure coming down the steps from the house. His features were as yet not at all clear to them for he was a dark silhouette against the glare of the setting sun reflected in the windows behind him. But as he came towards them all doubts and fears vanished, for the ginger beard was his, the long rolling stride was his and the voice they heard now belonged most certainly to their father.

'Sure you're a bit young to be travelling alone, aren't you?' he said, shielding his eyes against the sun. 'Only an hour or two before sundown and there's nowhere else for miles around.'

'Do you not recognise us?' Annie asked, getting to her feet. 'Do you not know who we are, Father?' And the moment she spoke, he did. He stood rooted to the spot, still not quite able to believe the evidence of his eyes and ears.

Annie spoke again. 'You gave us a terrible fright, Father,' she said, pointing down at the grave beside her. 'So who might that be then?'

''Tis Katey,' said her father. 'Do you not remember how the old dog ran away after me when I left home. Well, she stayed with me across from the East, came back to Ireland with me to look for you and then followed me all the way back here again. She never left my side in all that time. Worn out with living she was – died only last week.'

'We thought it was you in there, Father,' said Sean, and he ran and was first to reach him, burying his head in his father's shoulder. But Annie was not far behind and launched herself into his outstretched arm, and hung on round his neck. None of them wanted to let go and it was some moments before the tears were over and they could look at each other. Only then could they all fully accept the reality of their reunion.

'Patrick O'Brien,' came a voice from inside the house. 'Are you comin' with that wood for the oven or aren't you? Or do I fetch it in myself?'

'I'm comin', but 'tis somethin' better than wood I'll be bringing you, darlin',' laughed Patrick O'Brien, his smiling eyes not leaving his children's faces. Those eyes kindled the sudden new hope that surged inside them.

''Tis her voice, but it can't be her,' Annie said. 'Didn't we leave her for dead in Ireland? Oh, Father, she sent us away – we wouldn't have left her else.'

'I know, Annie, I know,' said her father. 'She was waiting there for me when I went back and she told me everything. I know all about Danny and Mary and little Joe, about your Will and how he saved you. 'Twas him that cared for her 'till I got home. I told you I would be back for you, didn't I now? We missed each other by no more than a few weeks – that's all it was. We must have sailed right by each other on the ocean and never known it. But you're here now, Jesus be thanked, you're here now. I'd given you up for dead, darlins, given you right up; but she hadn't, not your mother. She never gives up. She always said you'd be here one day and here you are.'

The door of the house opened wide. The children looked up and saw their mother standing framed in the doorway. 'Who is it you're talking to out there?' she said, peering into the sun; and then, 'Oh sweet Mary, Mother of God. They've come home, they've come home.'

''Tis her Sean,' Anne cried. ''Tis Mother. She's 'live and not dead in the least. She's 'live. I'm not dreaming all this, am I Sean?'

'Not unless I am,' said Sean. 'And I'm not.' And they ran to her open arms.

'And haven't they grown, the both of them?' said their mother when she had hugged them enough.

'See?' said Annie, triumphantly. 'Didn't I tell you they'd say just that, Sean? Have I ever been wrong, do you think?'

'Annie's not changed then,' said their mother.

'Not at all,' said Sean. 'Just grown a bit.'

'Not so much that I can't throw you high as the sun if I've a mind to, young lady,' said her father, swinging Annie into the air above him.

'Take care you don't crush the torc,' said Annie, laughing down at him. 'Sure it's worked terrible hard to get us here. 'Twould be an awful shame to squash it now.' And she went on in a quieter voice. 'Little Luke said we'd find you, Father.'

'And Seamus Finn and the Colonel,' said Sean. 'They all told us we'd get here.'

'And who might they be?' asked their father.

'And where did you come by that old fiddle case, Sean?' said his mother, walking up the steps with her arm around him.

'Well, 'tis a long story, Mother,' said Sean. 'A long, long story.'